MERMAID DAYS™

The Sunken Ship

Read the next MERMAID DAYS book!

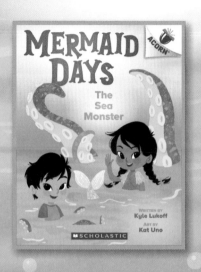

MERMAID DAYS

The Sea Monster

ACORN

WRITTEN BY
Kyle Lukoff

ART BY
Kat Uno

SCHOLASTIC

MERMAID DAYS™

The Sunken Ship

WRITTEN BY
Kyle Lukoff

ART BY
Kat Uno

ACORN™
SCHOLASTIC INC.

To Saba Sulaiman: I don't know where I'd be without you.
—KL

For all those out there who truly believe that mermaids exist.
—KU

Text copyright © 2022 by Kyle Lukoff
Illustrations copyright © 2022 by Kat Uno

Library of Congress Cataloging-in-Publication Data

Names: Lukoff, Kyle, author. | Uno, Kat, illustrator.
Title: The sunken ship / by Kyle Lukoff ; illustrated by Kat Uno.
Description: First edition. | New York Acorn/Scholastic, 2022. |
Series: Mermaid days 1
Summary: Vera the mermaid and her half-octopus friend Beaker go on playful adventures in the underwater town of Tidal Grove. |
Identifiers: LCCN 2021013036 | ISBN 9781338794595 (paperback) | ISBN 9781338794601 (library binding)
Subjects: CYAC: Mermaids—Fiction. | Marine animals—Fiction. | Friendship—Fiction.
Classification: LCC PZ7.1.L8456 Su 2022 | DDC [E]—dc23
LC record available at https://lccn.loc.gov/2021013036

10 9 8 7 6 5 4 3 2   22 23 24 25 26

Printed in China   62
First edition, May 2022
Edited by Rachel Matson
Book design by Jaime Lucero

TABLE OF CONTENTS

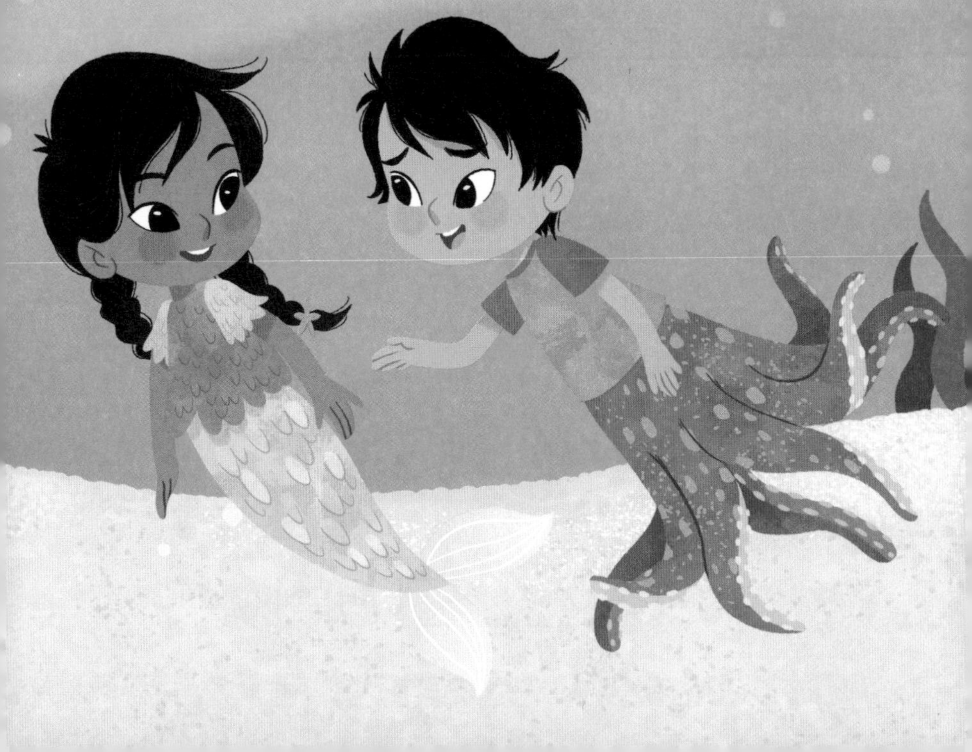

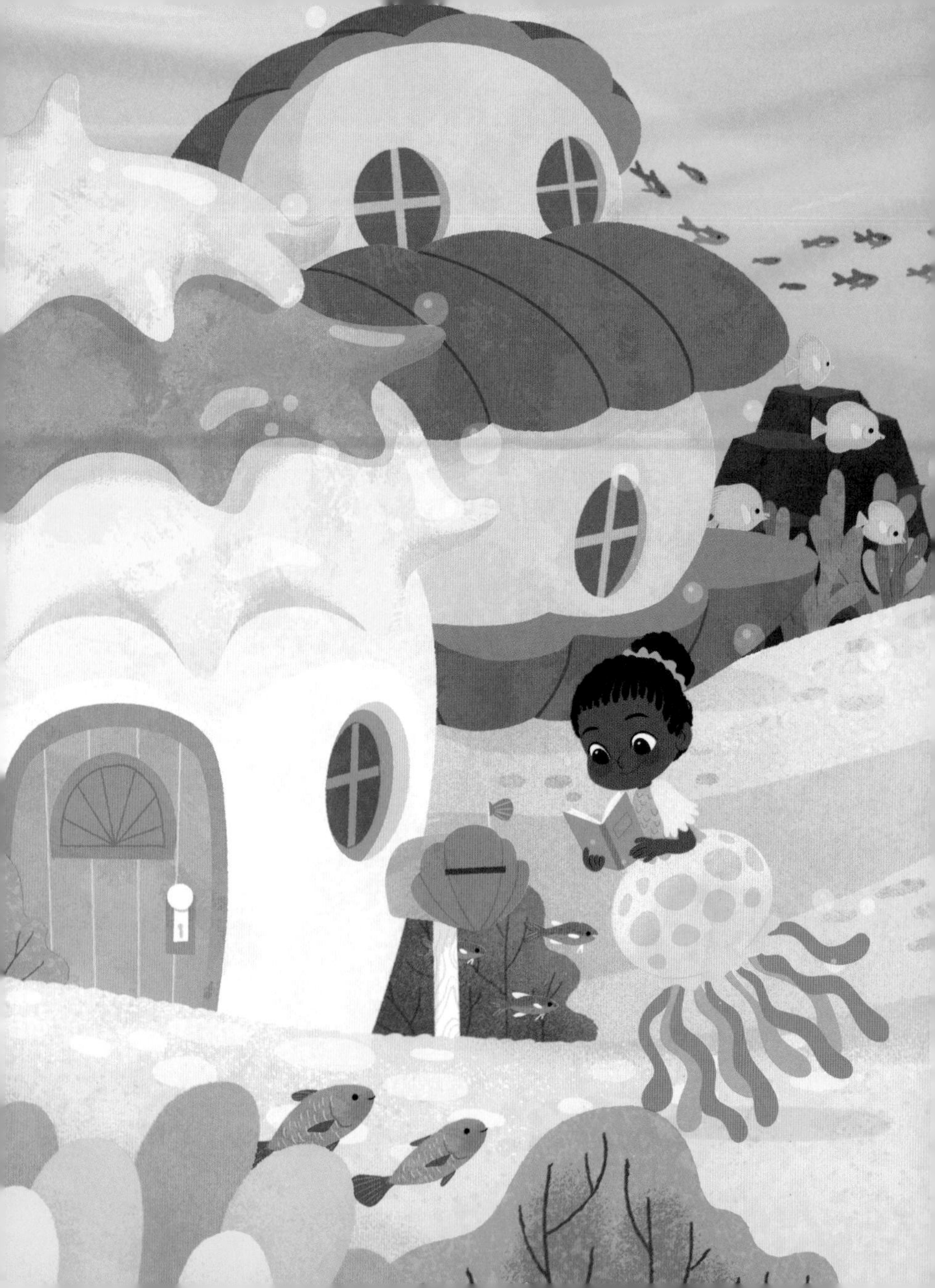
1

MEET VERA

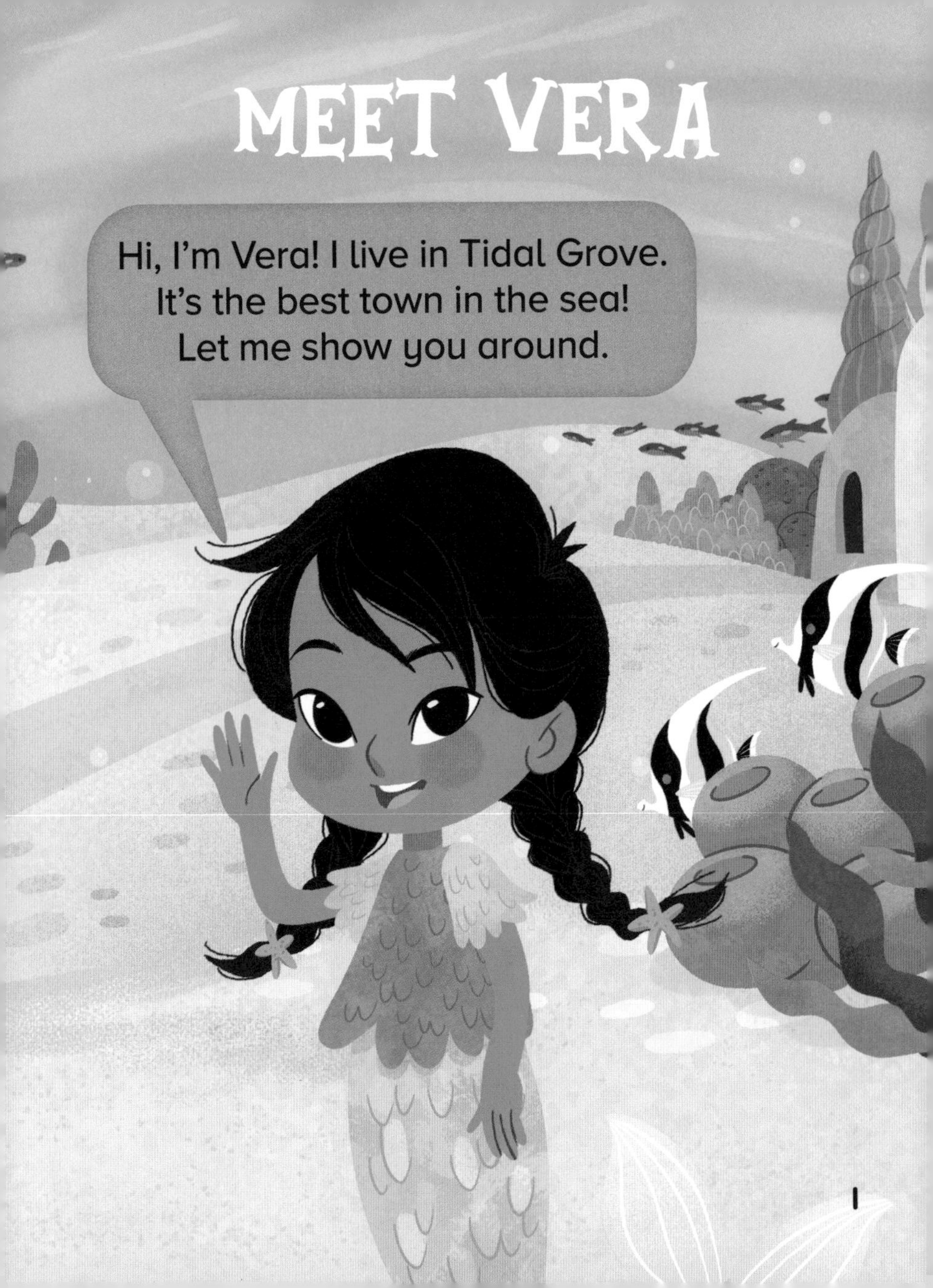
Hi, I'm Vera! I live in Tidal Grove. It's the best town in the sea! Let me show you around.

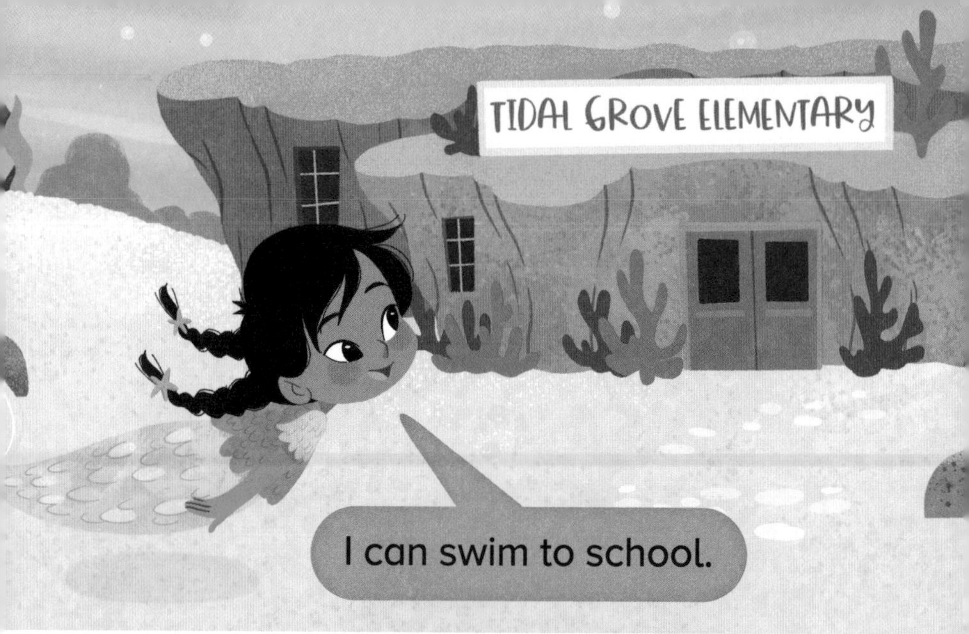
TIDAL GROVE ELEMENTARY
I can swim to school.

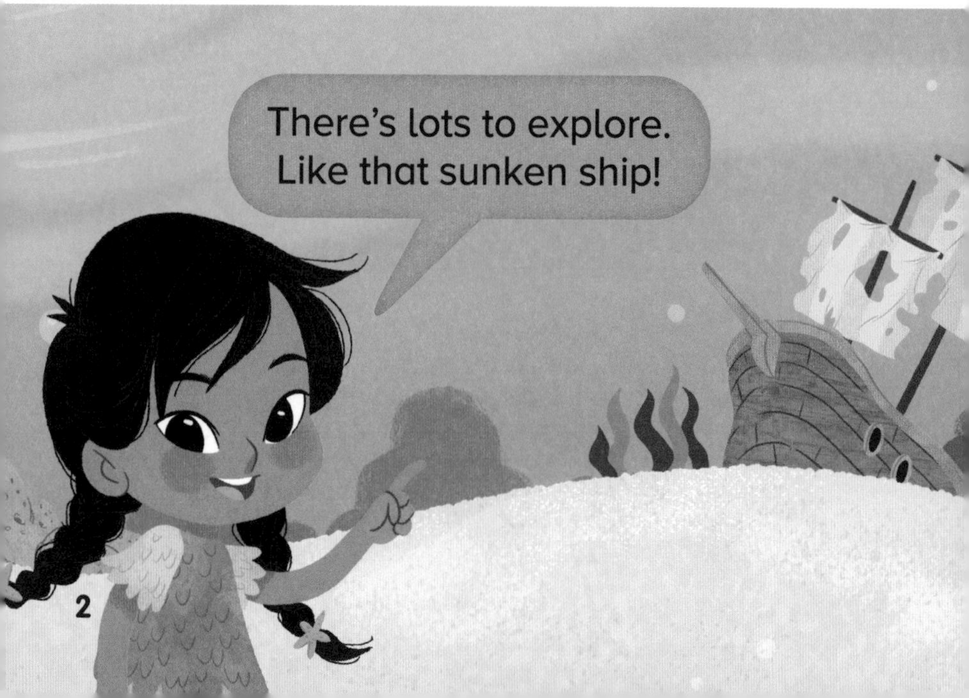
There's lots to explore.
Like that sunken ship!

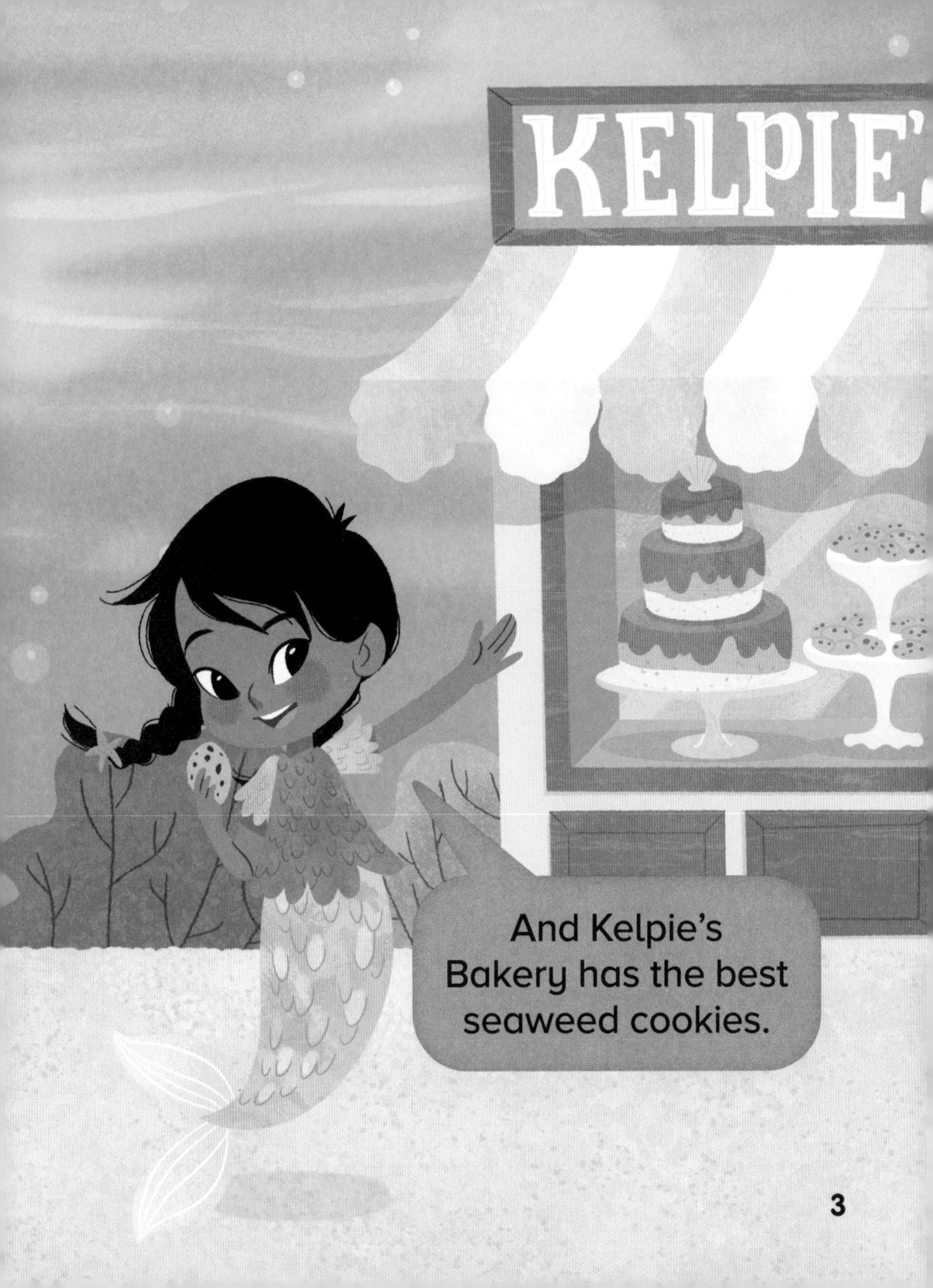
KELPIE'
And Kelpie's Bakery has the best seaweed cookies.

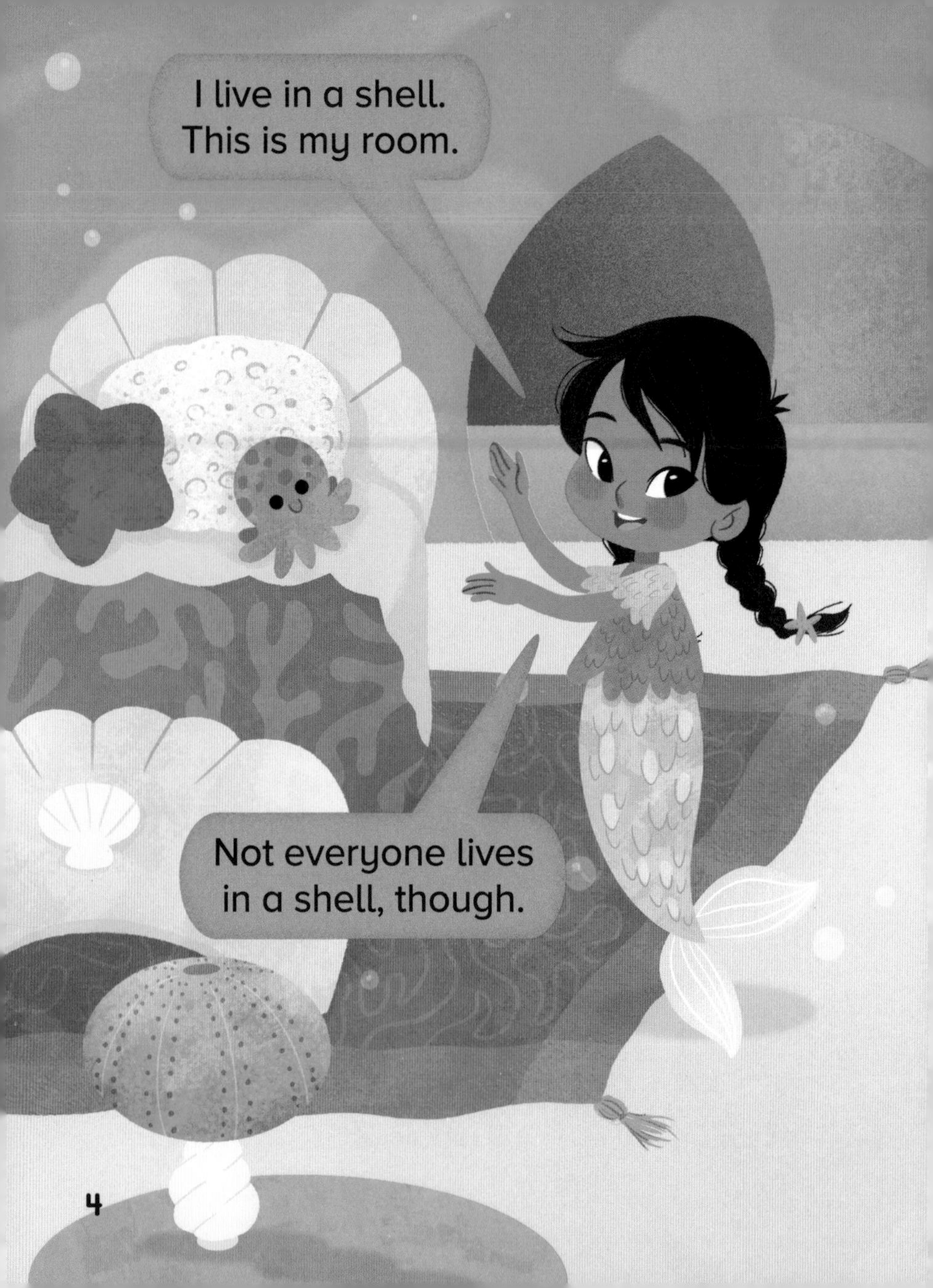
I live in a shell.
This is my room.
Not everyone lives
in a shell, though.

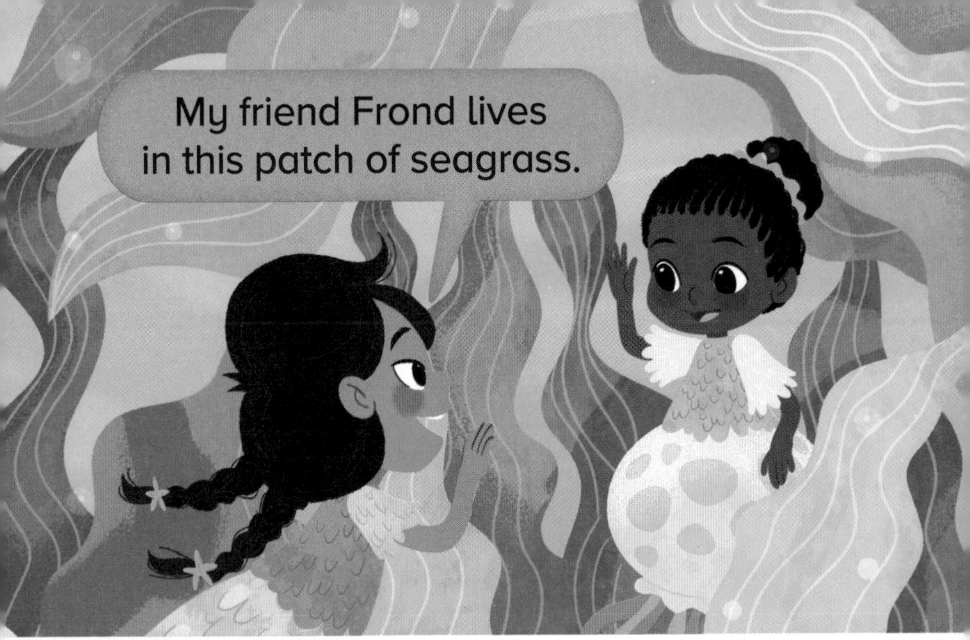
My friend Frond lives in this patch of seagrass.

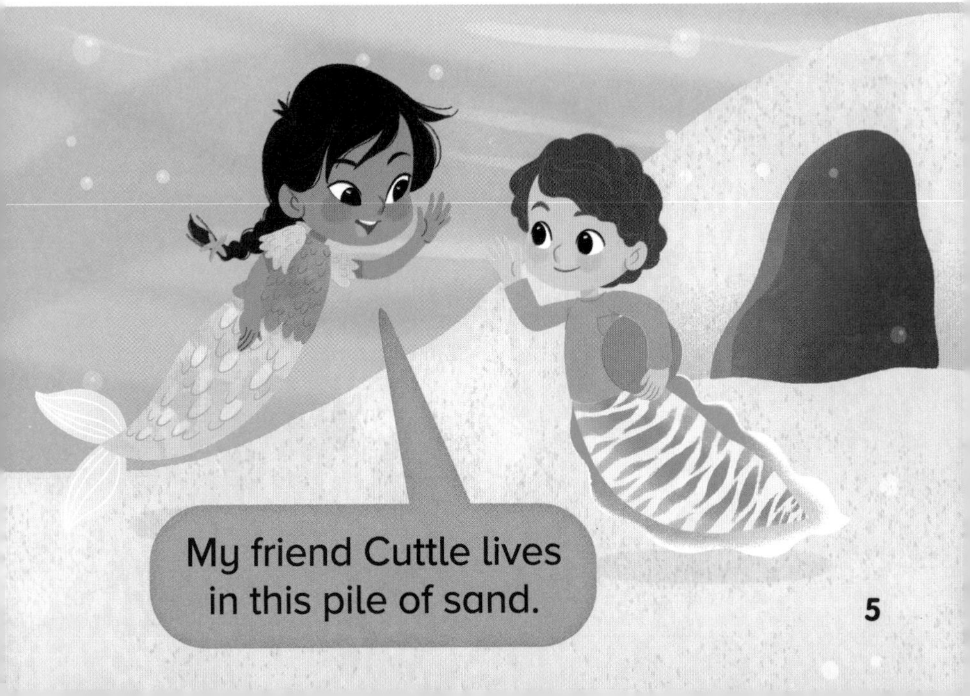
My friend Cuttle lives in this pile of sand.

Lots of my friends live in the coral reef.
It's the busiest place in town.

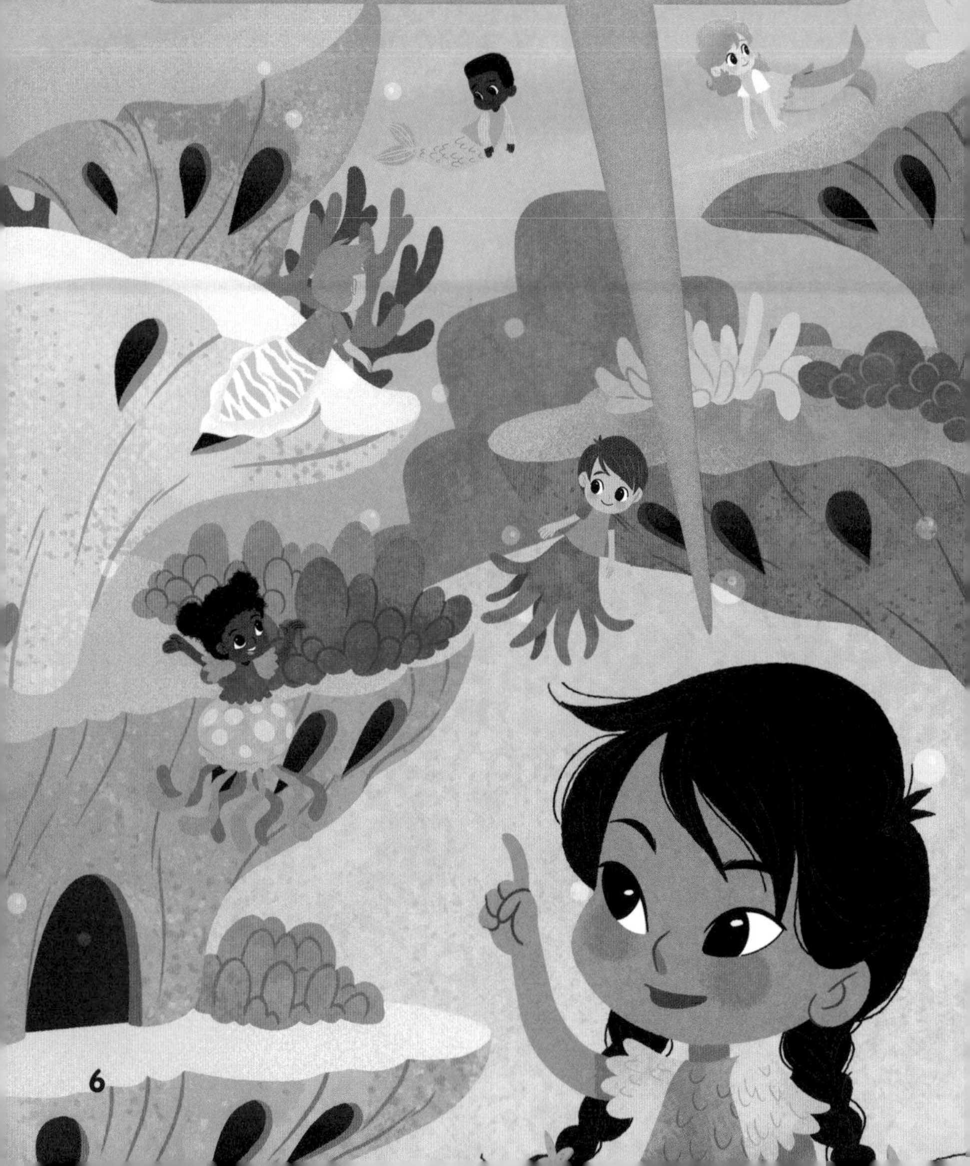

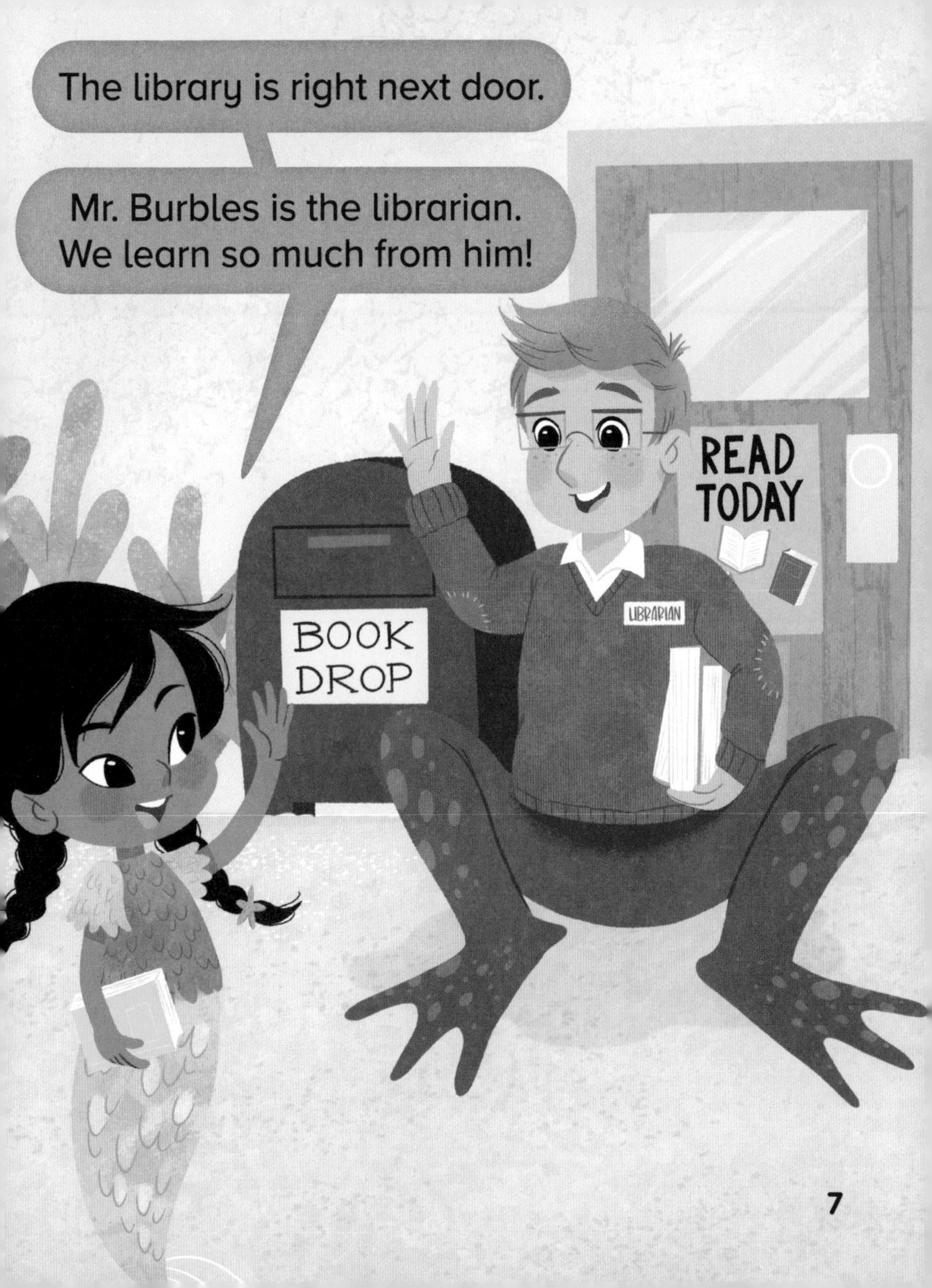
The library is right next door.
Mr. Burbles is the librarian. We learn so much from him!
READ TODAY
BOOK DROP
LIBRARIAN

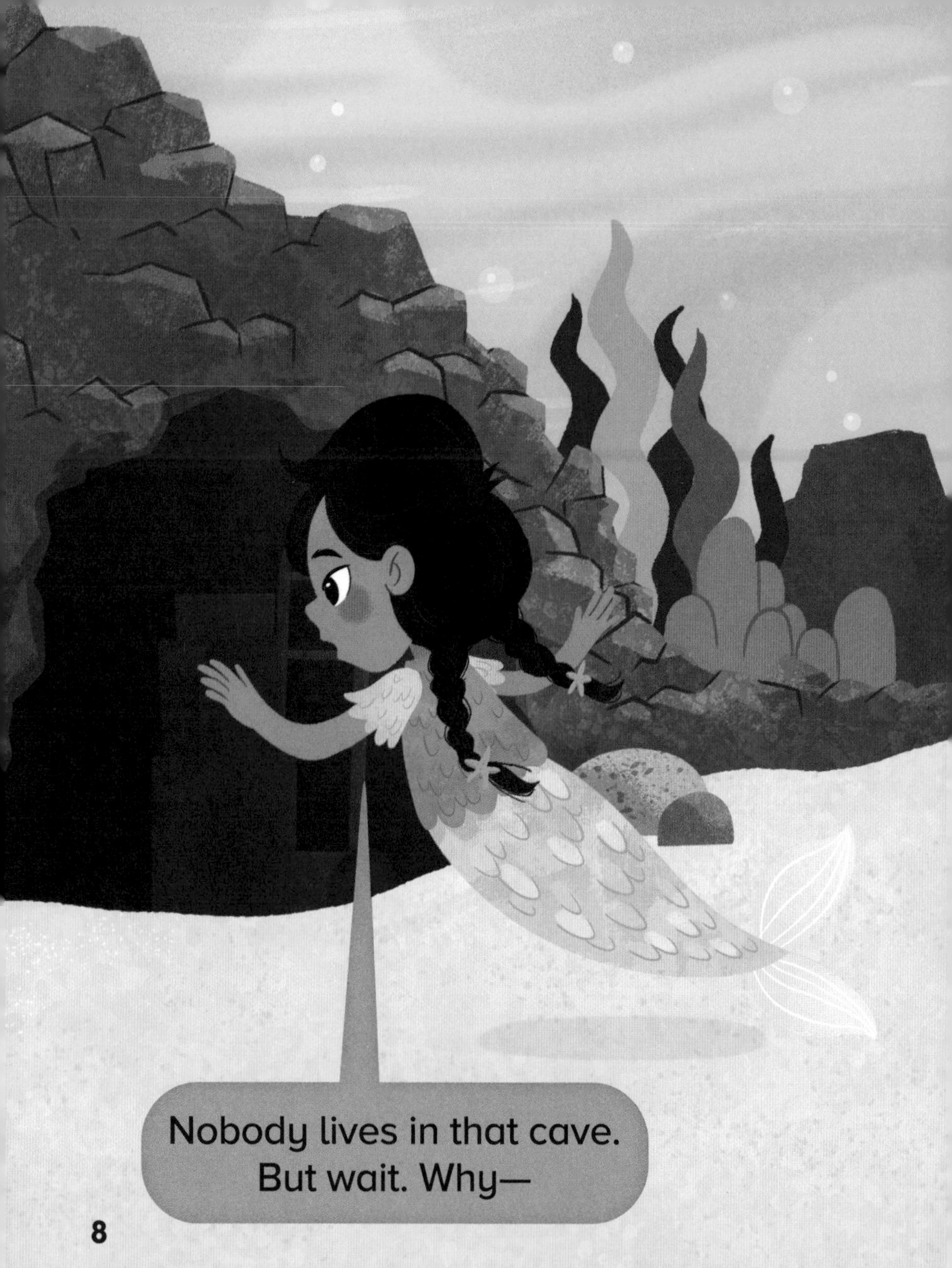
Nobody lives in that cave.
But wait. Why—

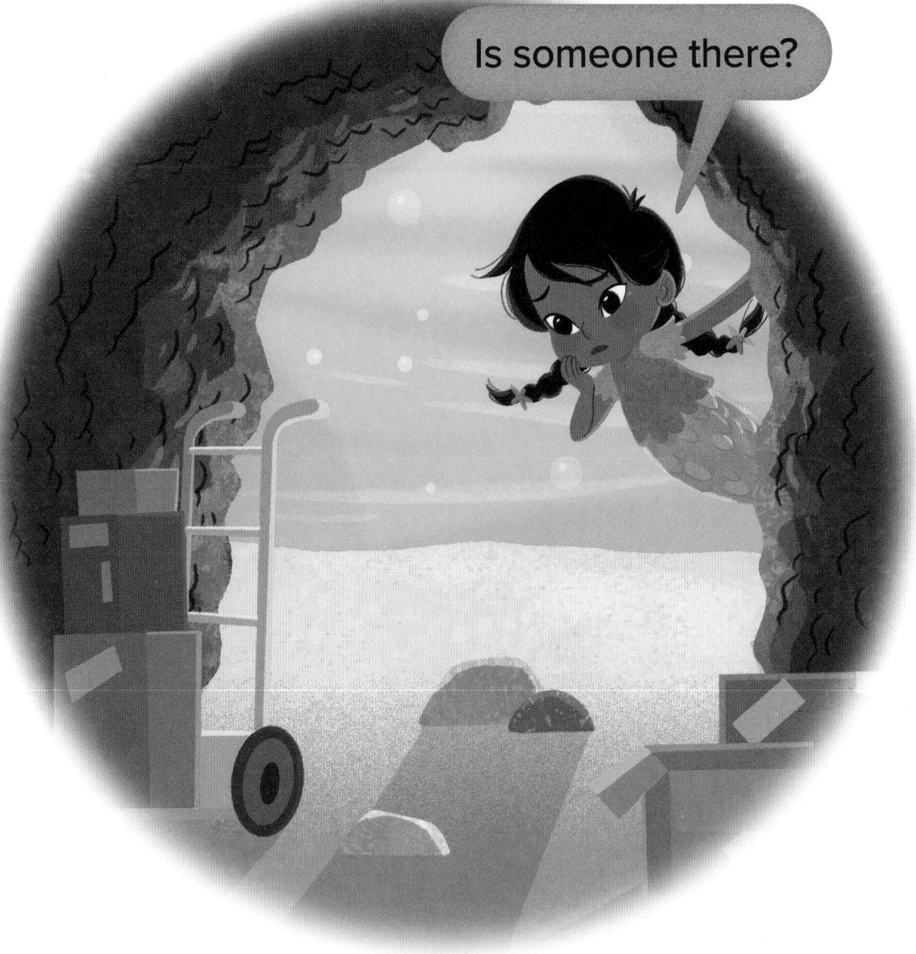
Is someone there?

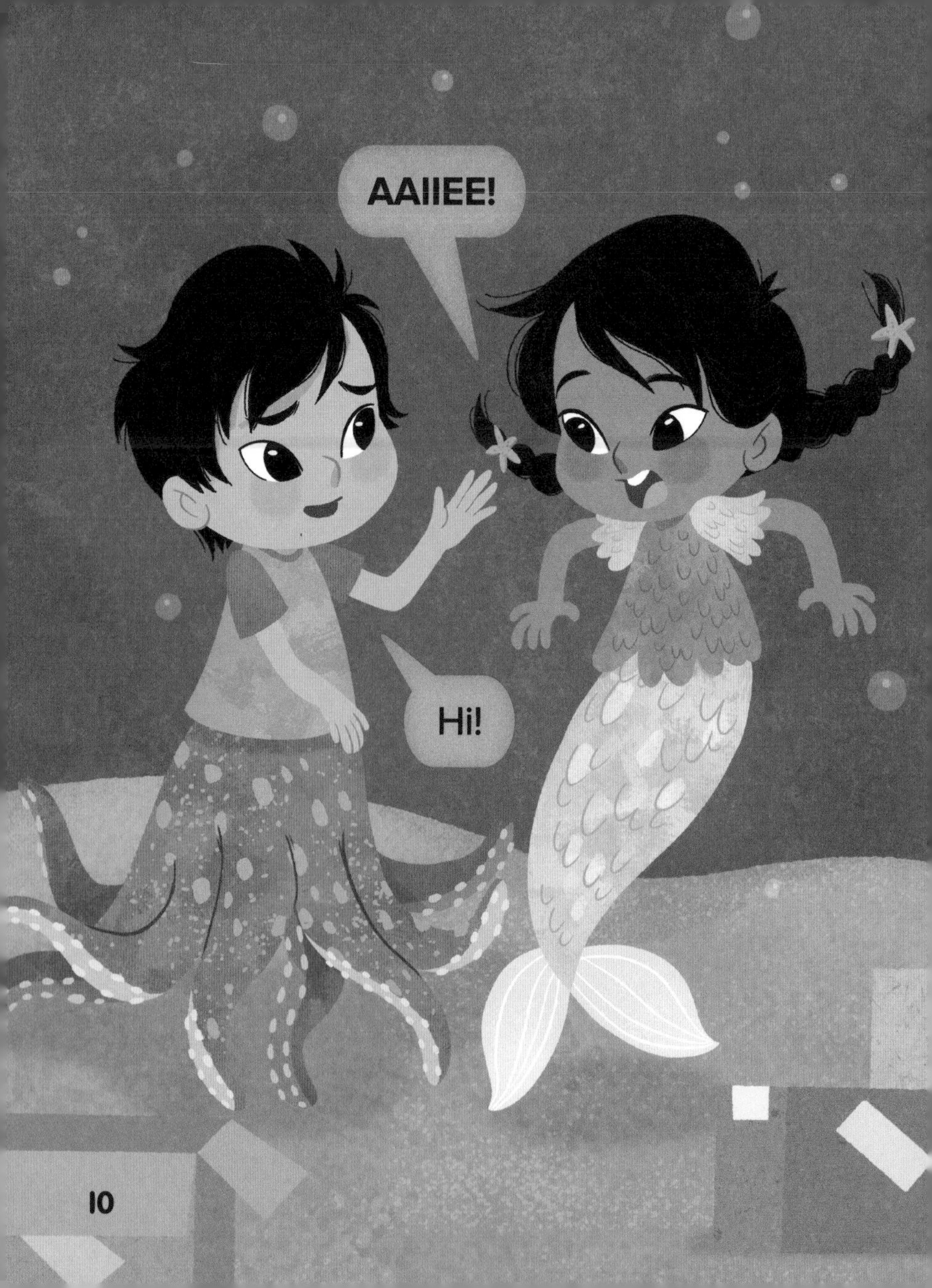
AAIIEE!
Hi!

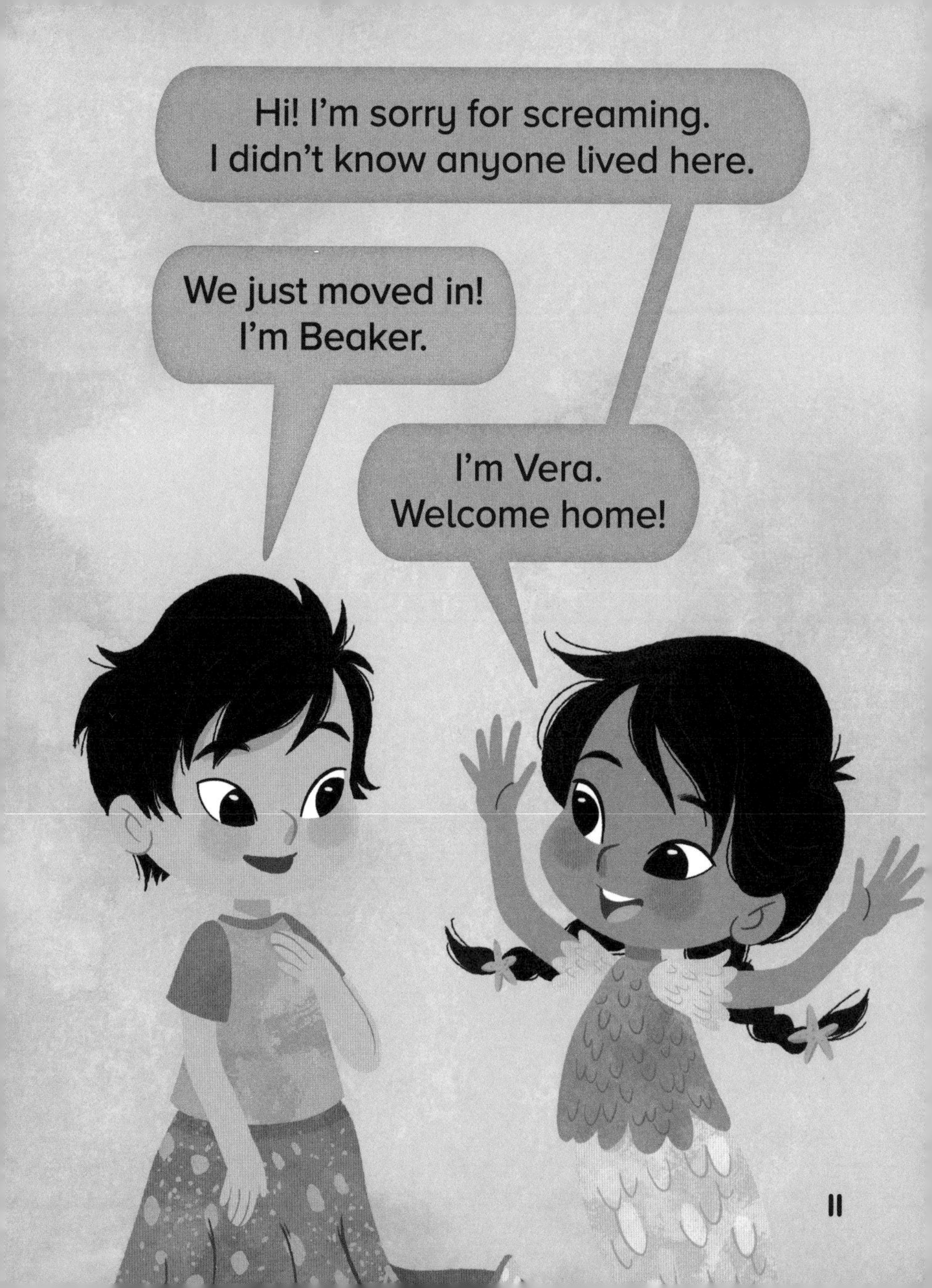
Hi! I'm sorry for screaming. I didn't know anyone lived here.
We just moved in! I'm Beaker.
I'm Vera. Welcome home!

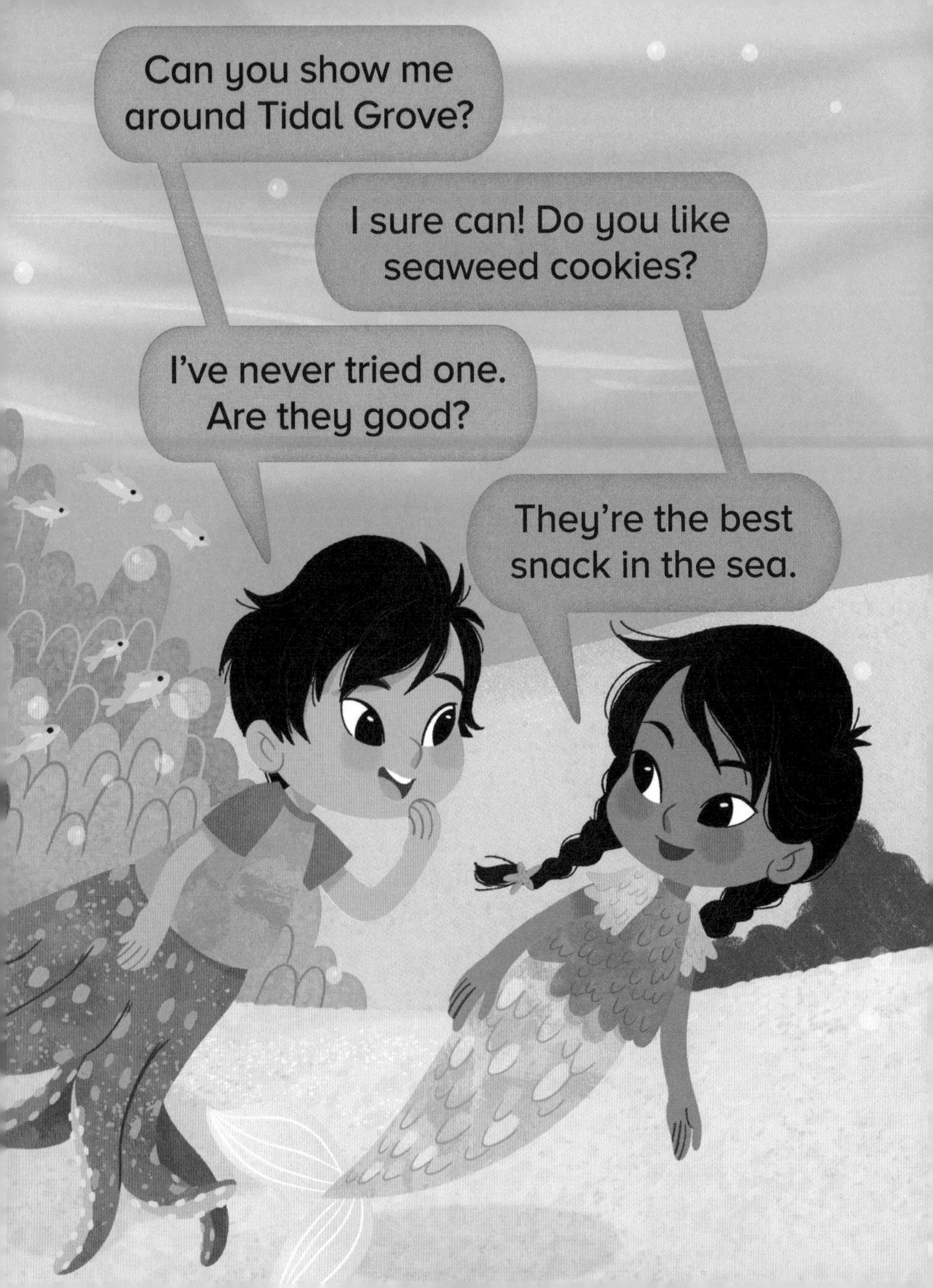
Can you show me around Tidal Grove?
I sure can! Do you like seaweed cookies?
I've never tried one. Are they good?
They're the best snack in the sea.

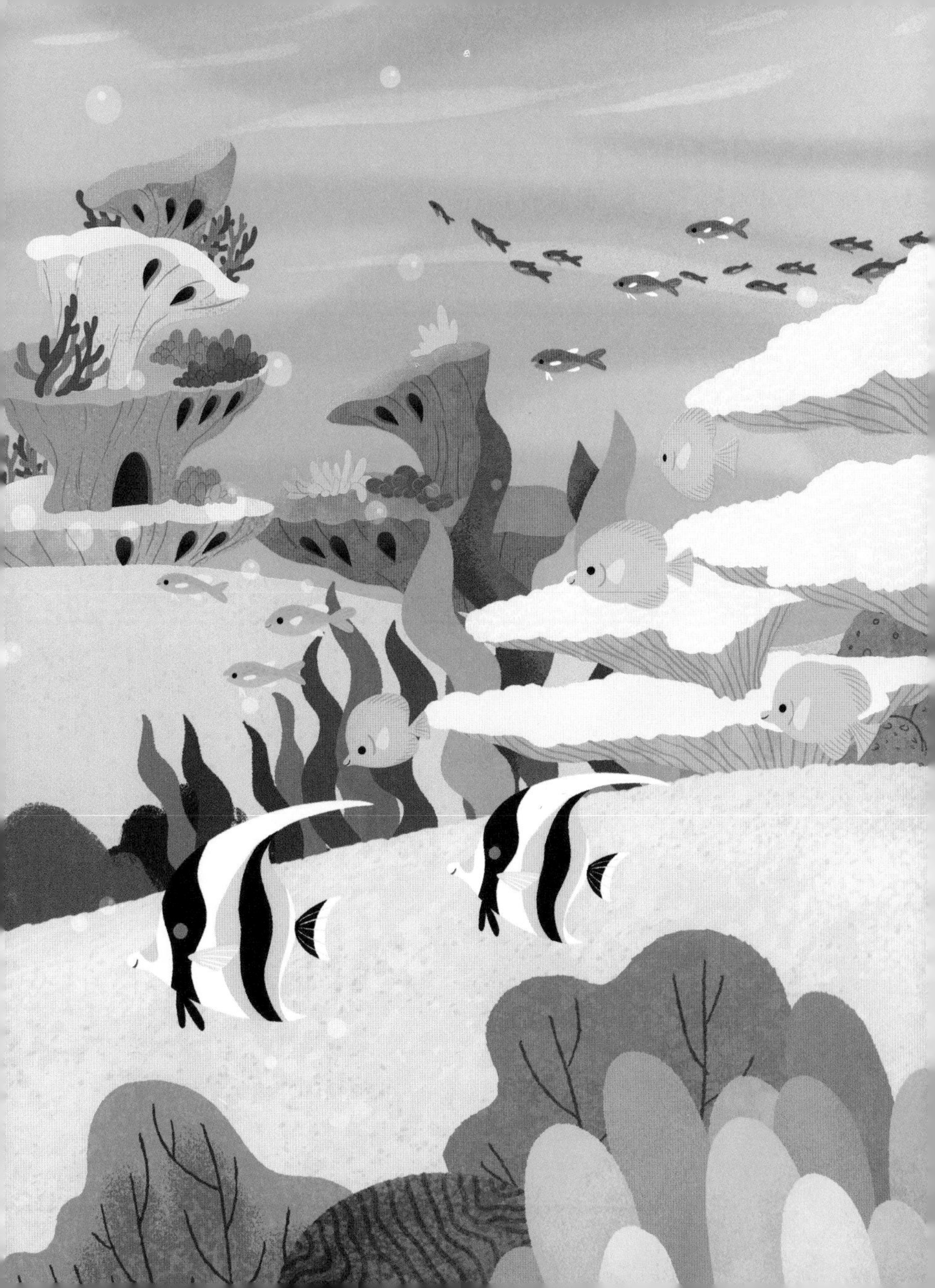

DID YOU KNOW?

Humans have cells in their brains called neurons ("NURR-ons").

Octopuses have those same cells in their legs!

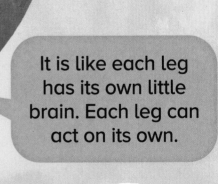

It is like each leg has its own little brain. Each leg can act on its own.

LIBRARIAN

BEAKER'S LEGS

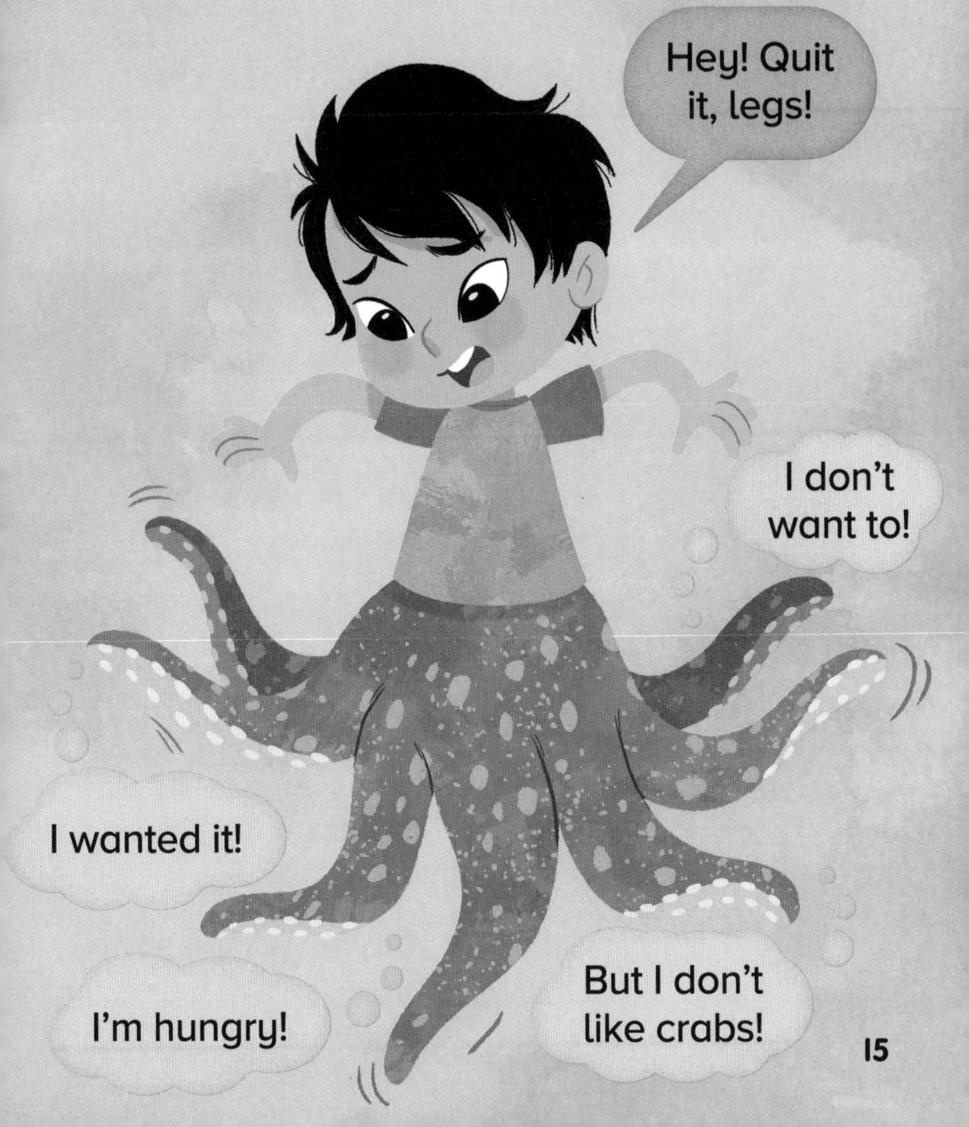

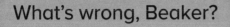

What's wrong, Beaker?

My legs aren't getting along. You know what those days are like, right?

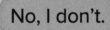

No, I don't.

16

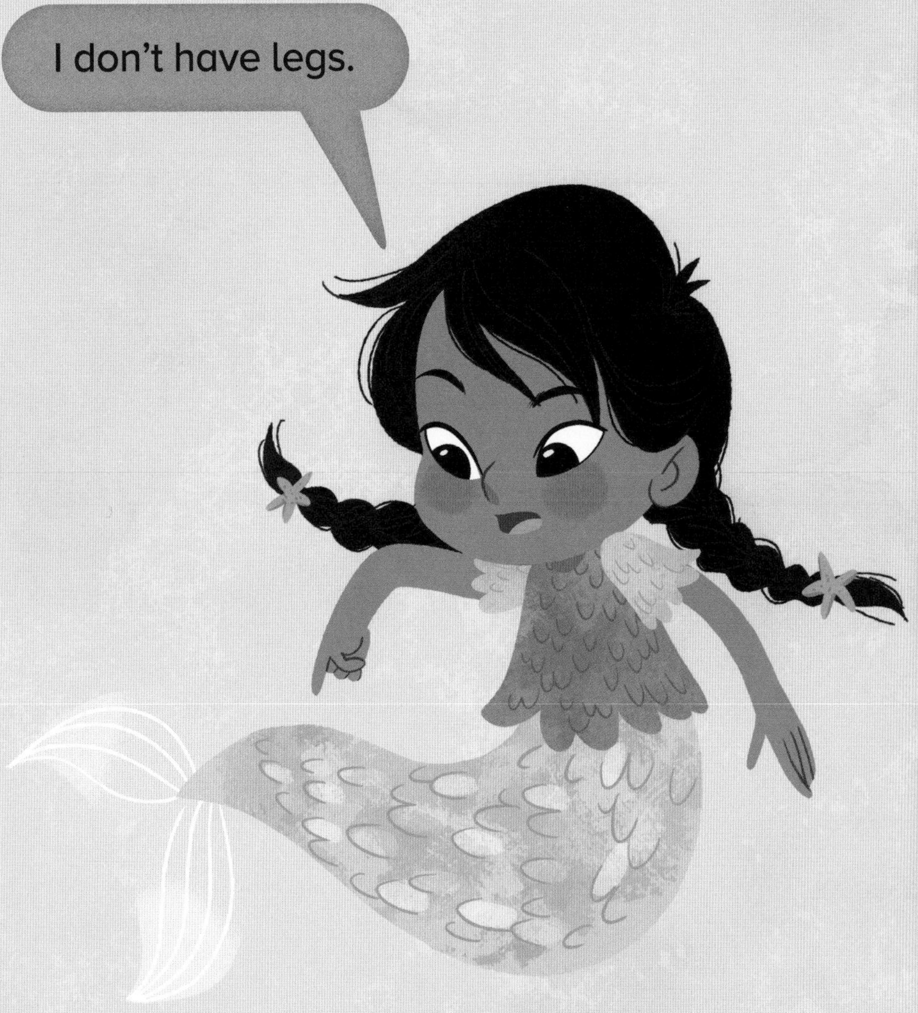
I don't have legs.

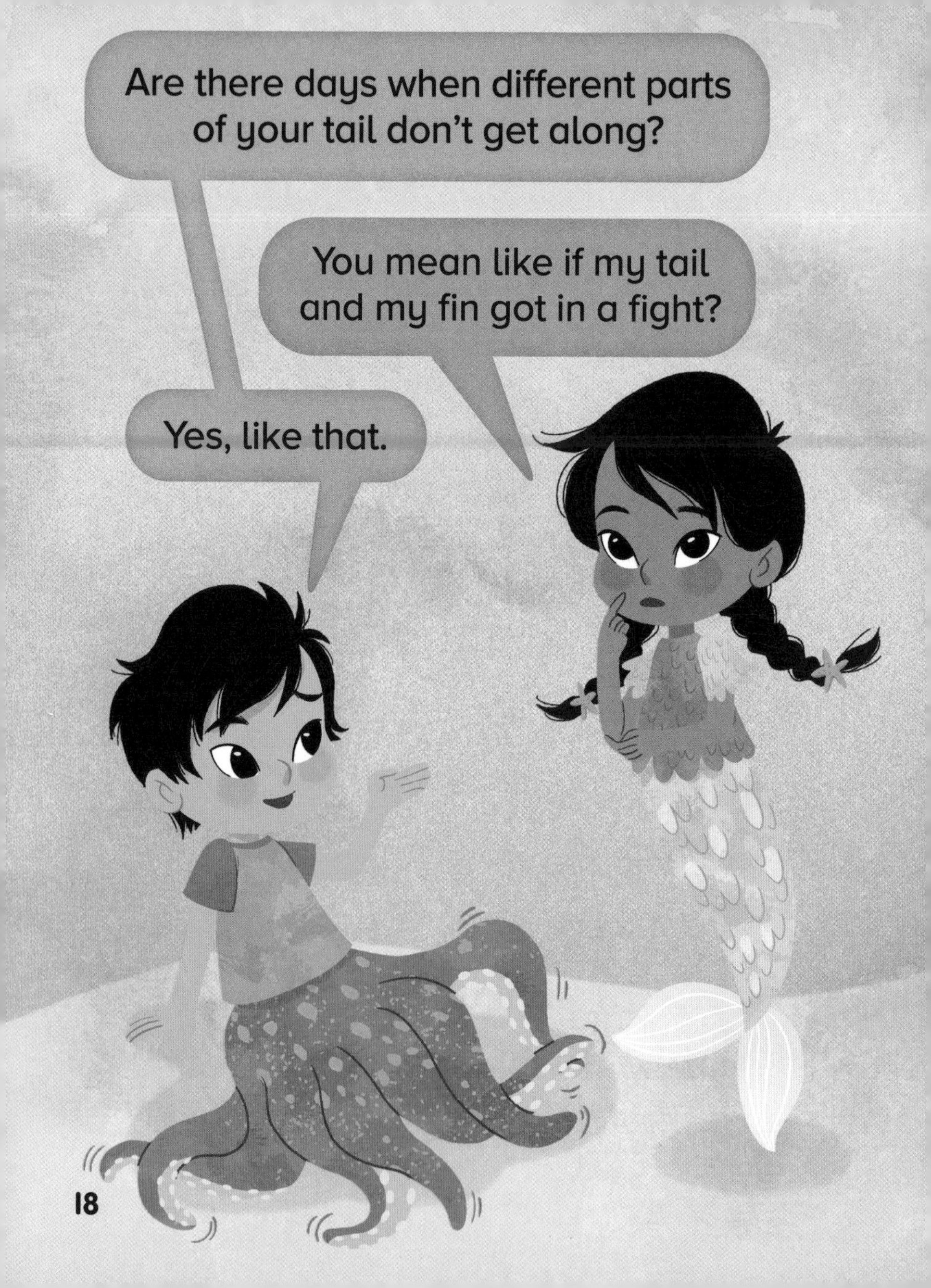
Are there days when different parts of your tail don't get along?
You mean like if my tail and my fin got in a fight?
Yes, like that.

No. That doesn't happen to me.
My tail is a tail. It's just more of me.

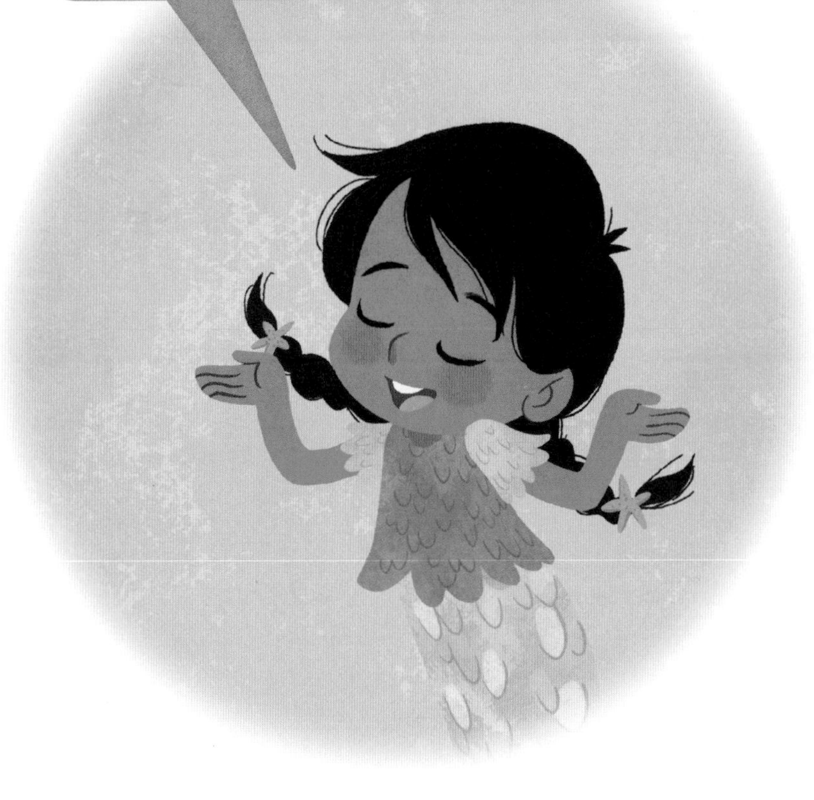

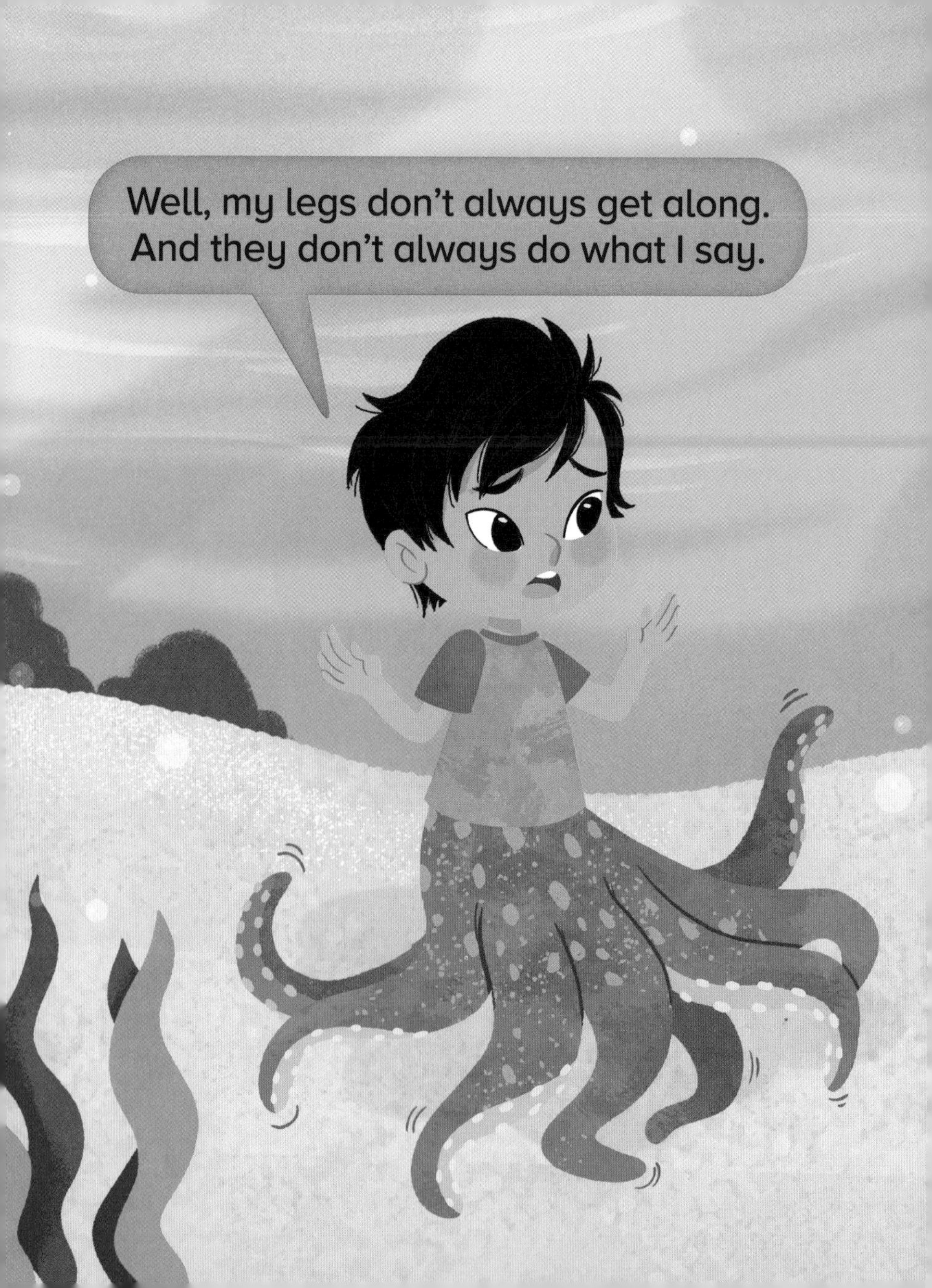
Well, my legs don't always get along.
And they don't always do what I say.

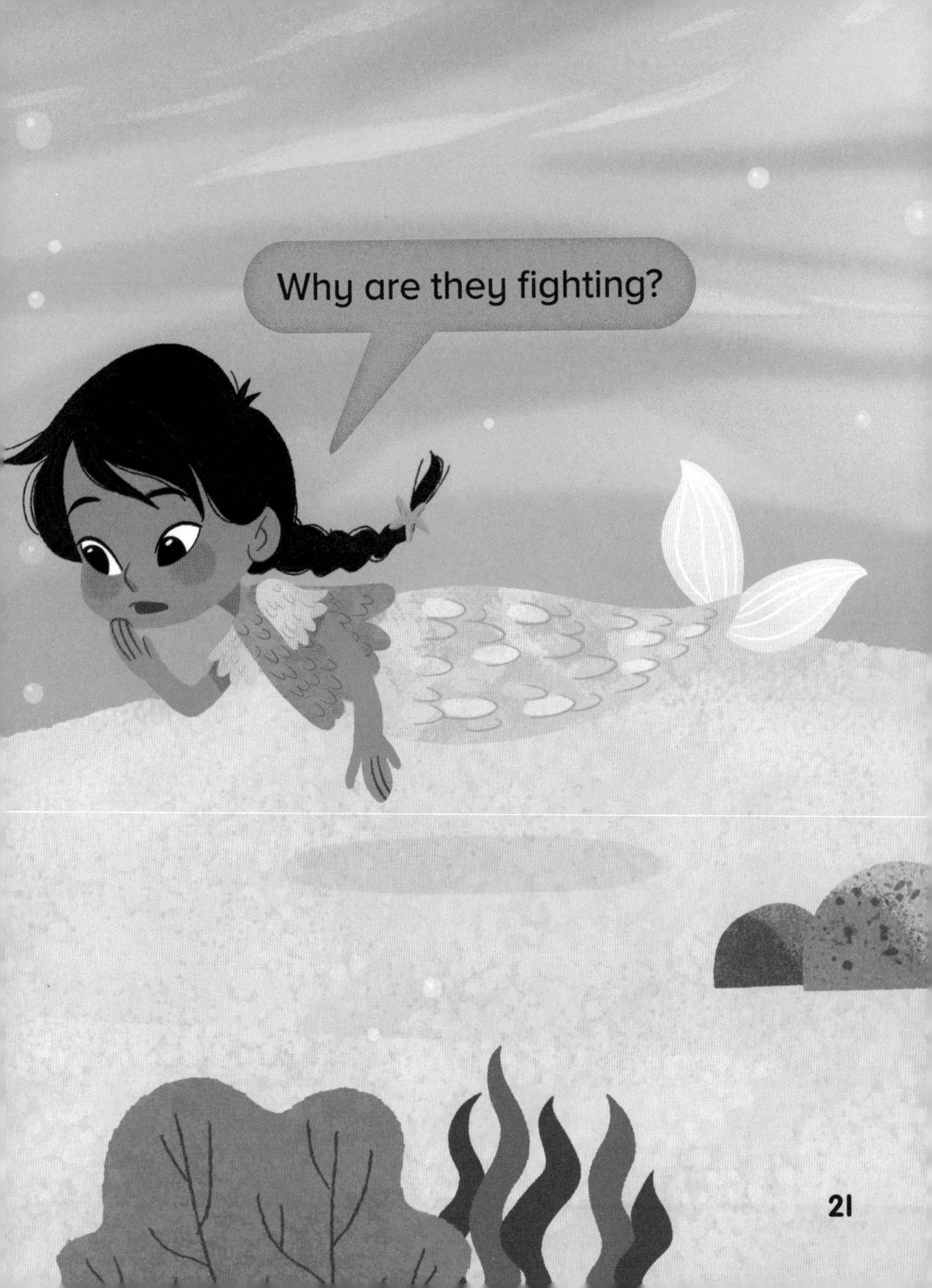
Why are they fighting?

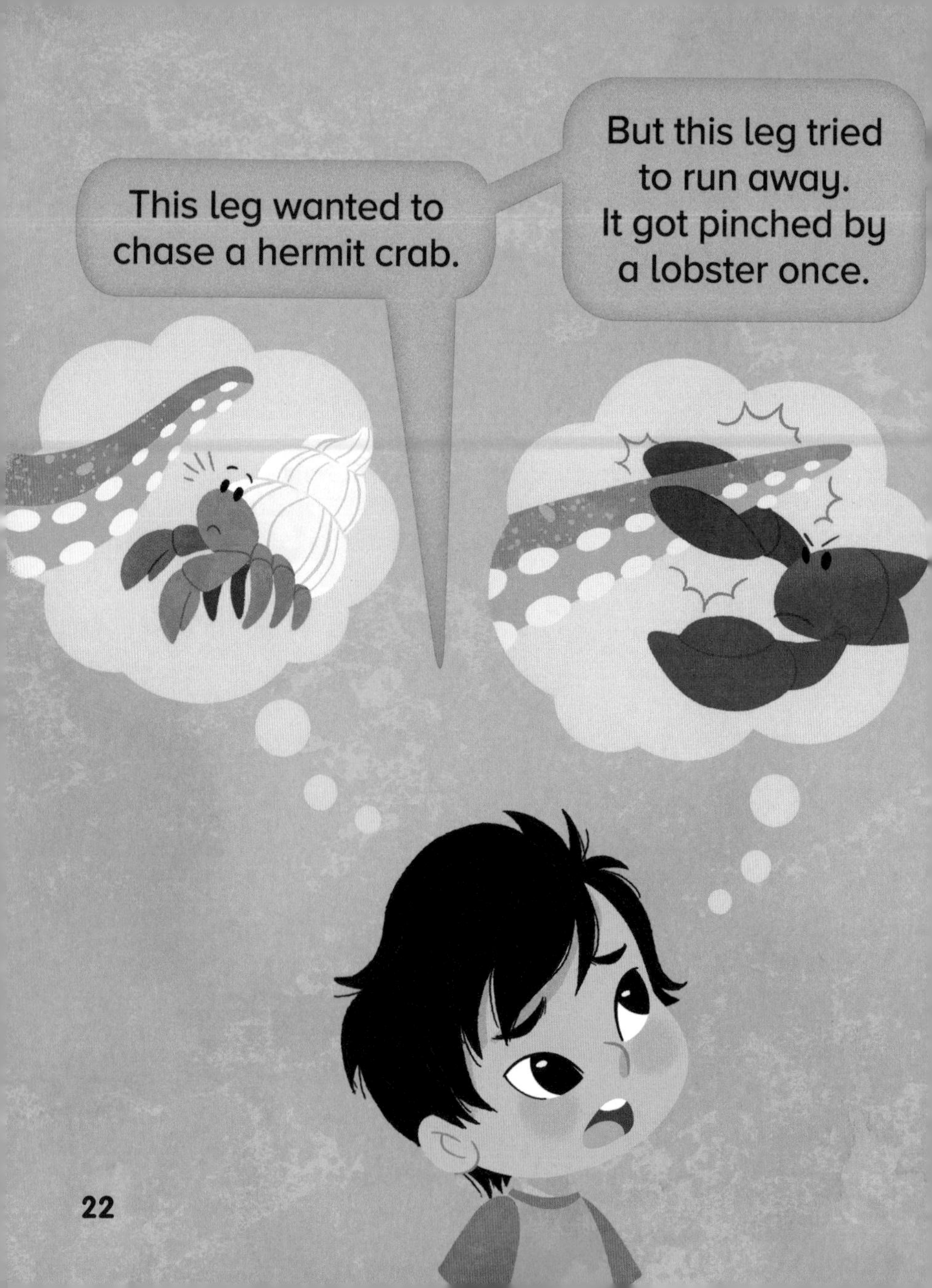
This leg wanted to chase a hermit crab.
But this leg tried to run away. It got pinched by a lobster once.

The other legs couldn't agree on who to follow.

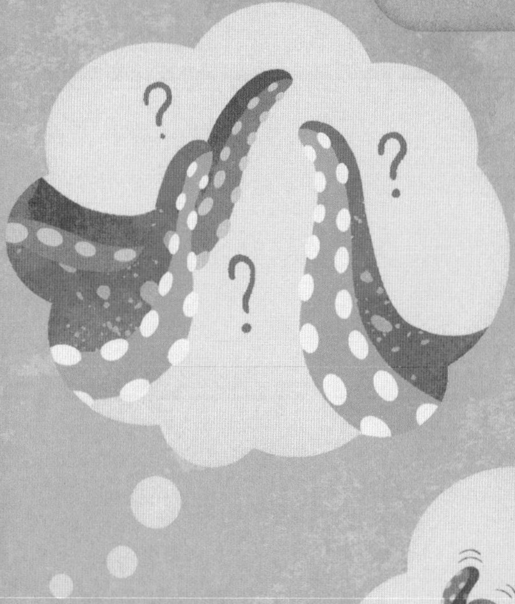

I got tangled up in the middle.

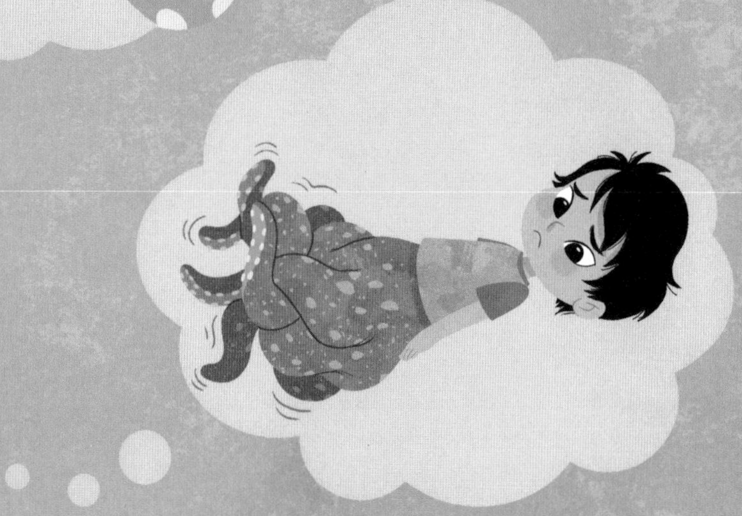

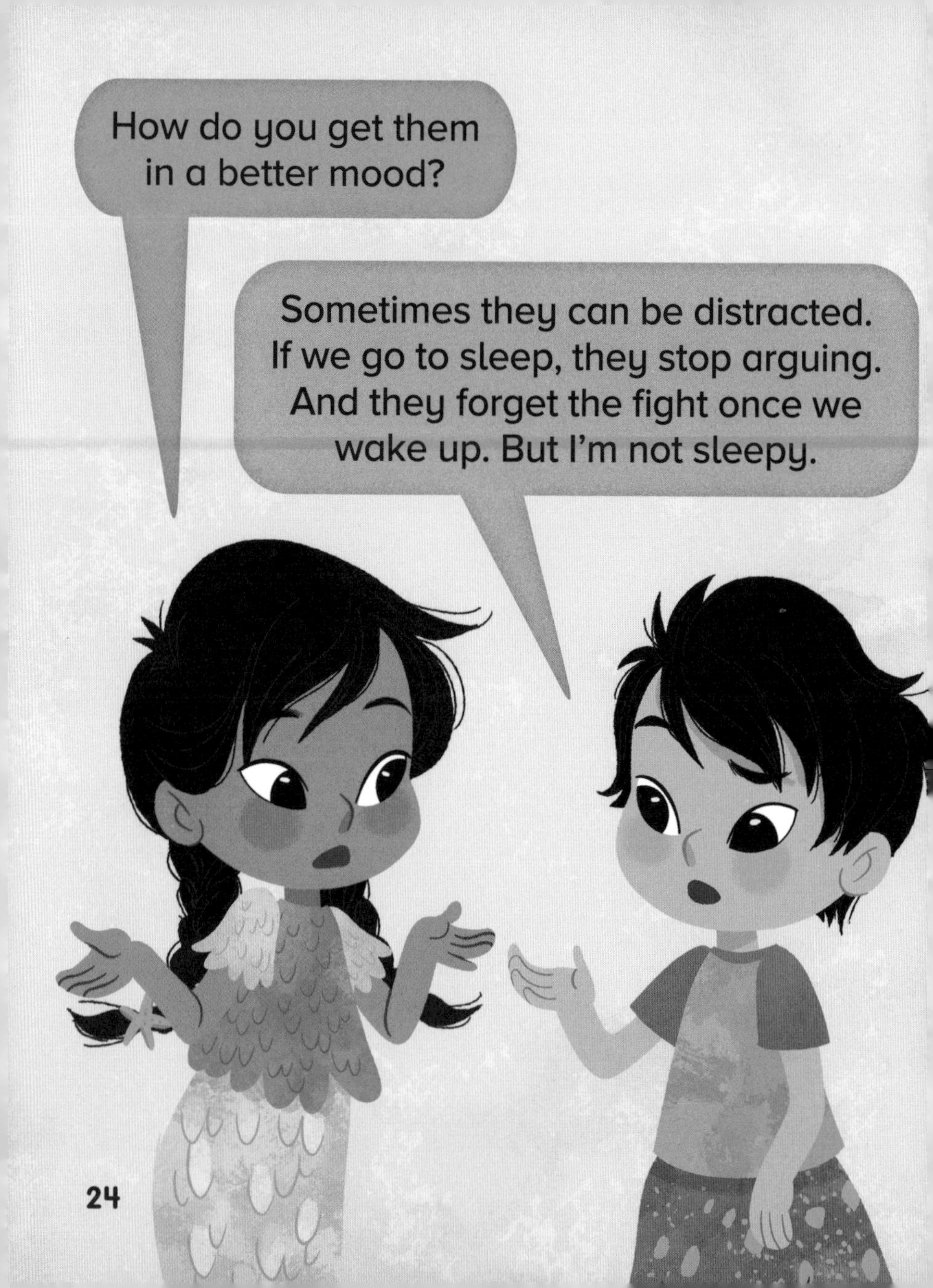
How do you get them in a better mood?
Sometimes they can be distracted. If we go to sleep, they stop arguing. And they forget the fight once we wake up. But I'm not sleepy.

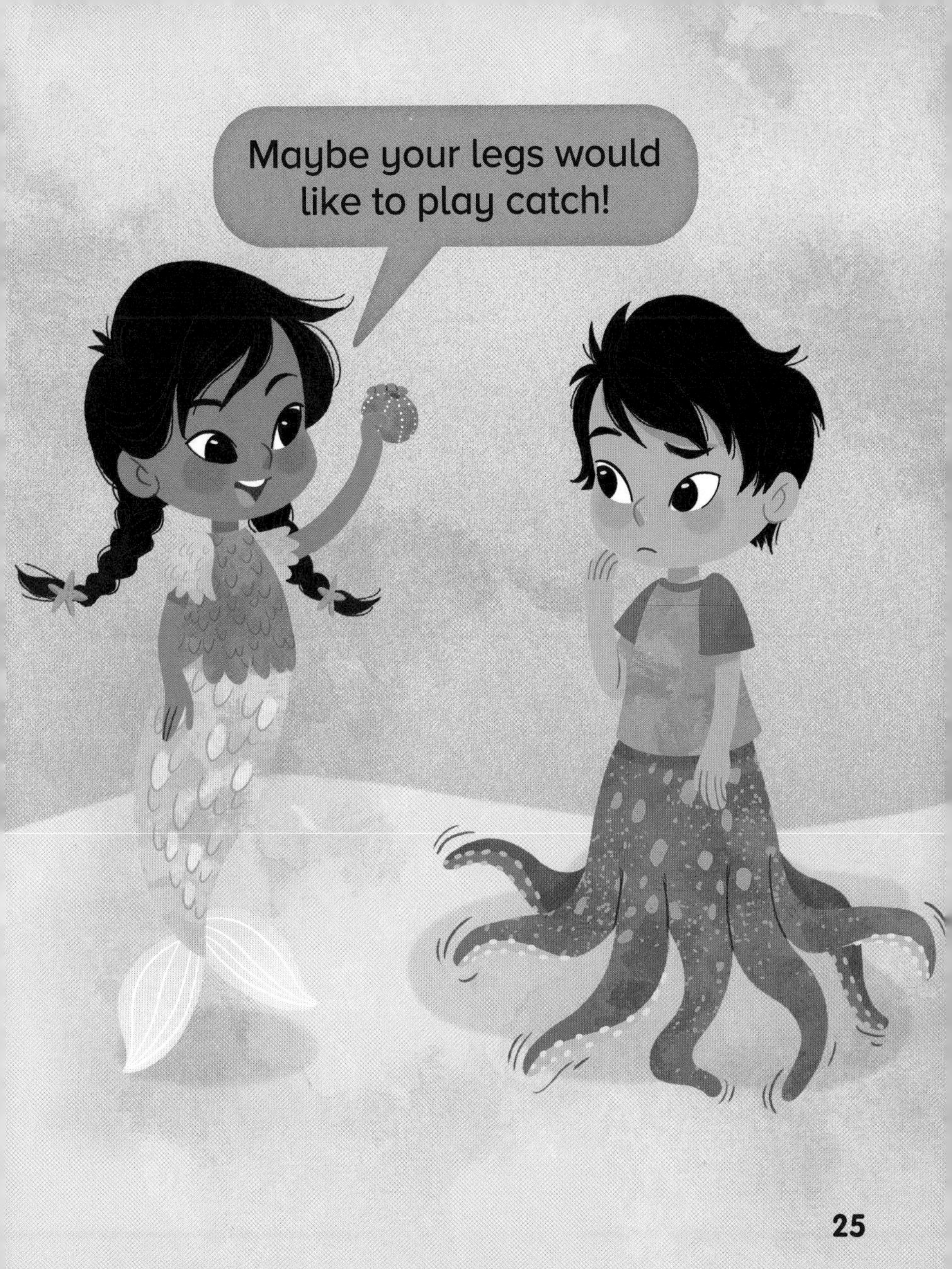
Maybe your legs would like to play catch!

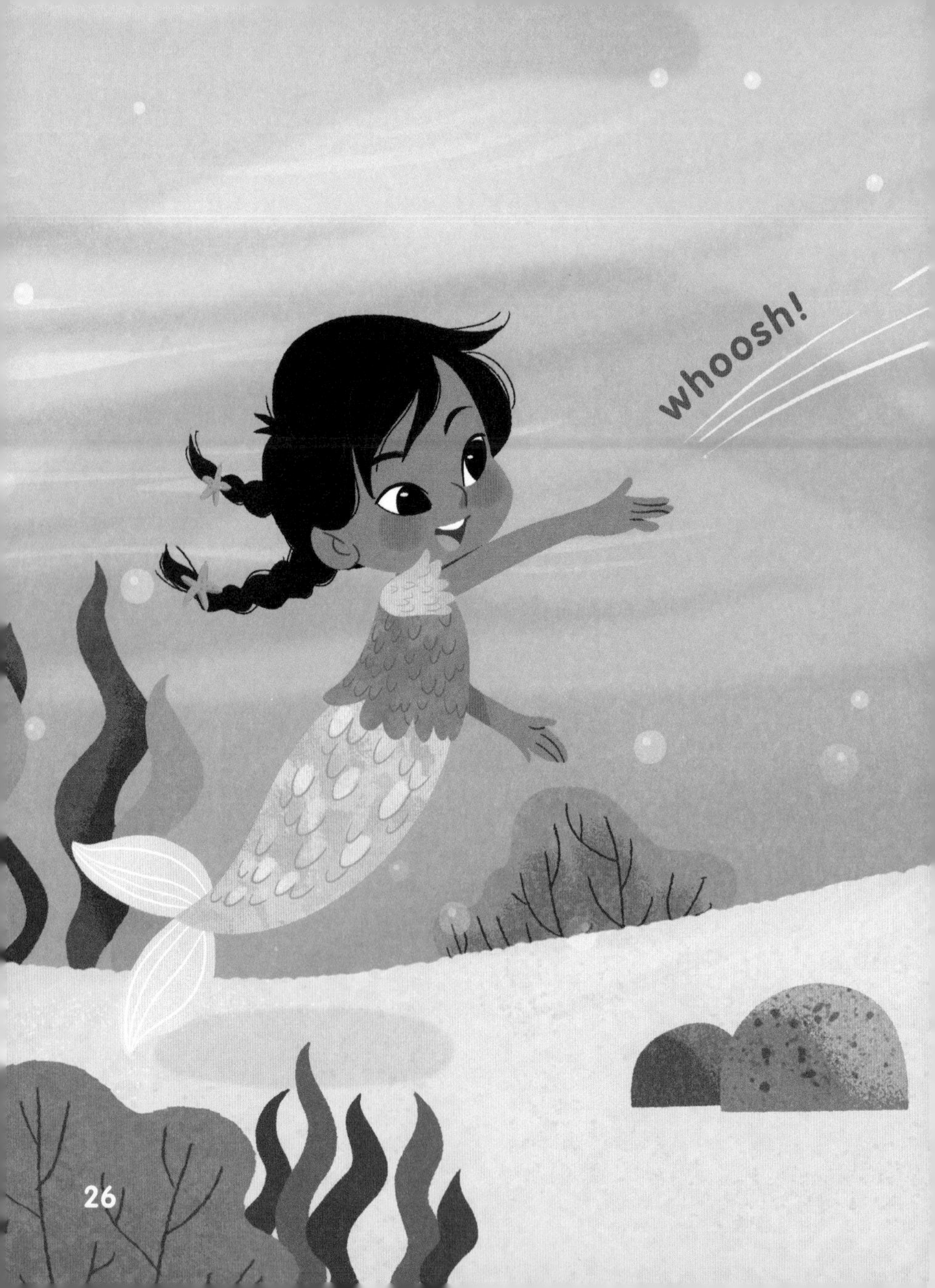
whoosh!

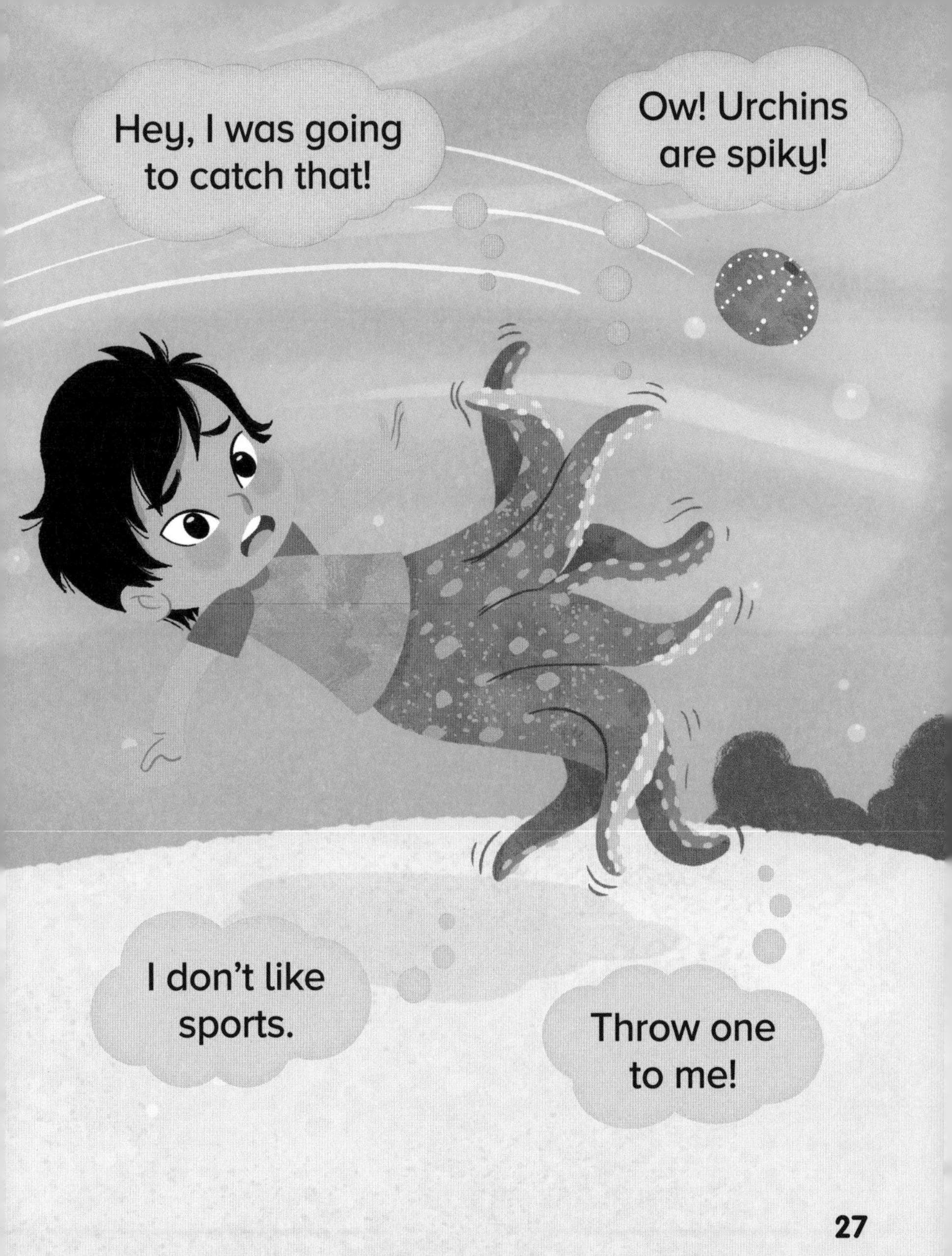
Hey, I was going to catch that!
Ow! Urchins are spiky!
I don't like sports.
Throw one to me!

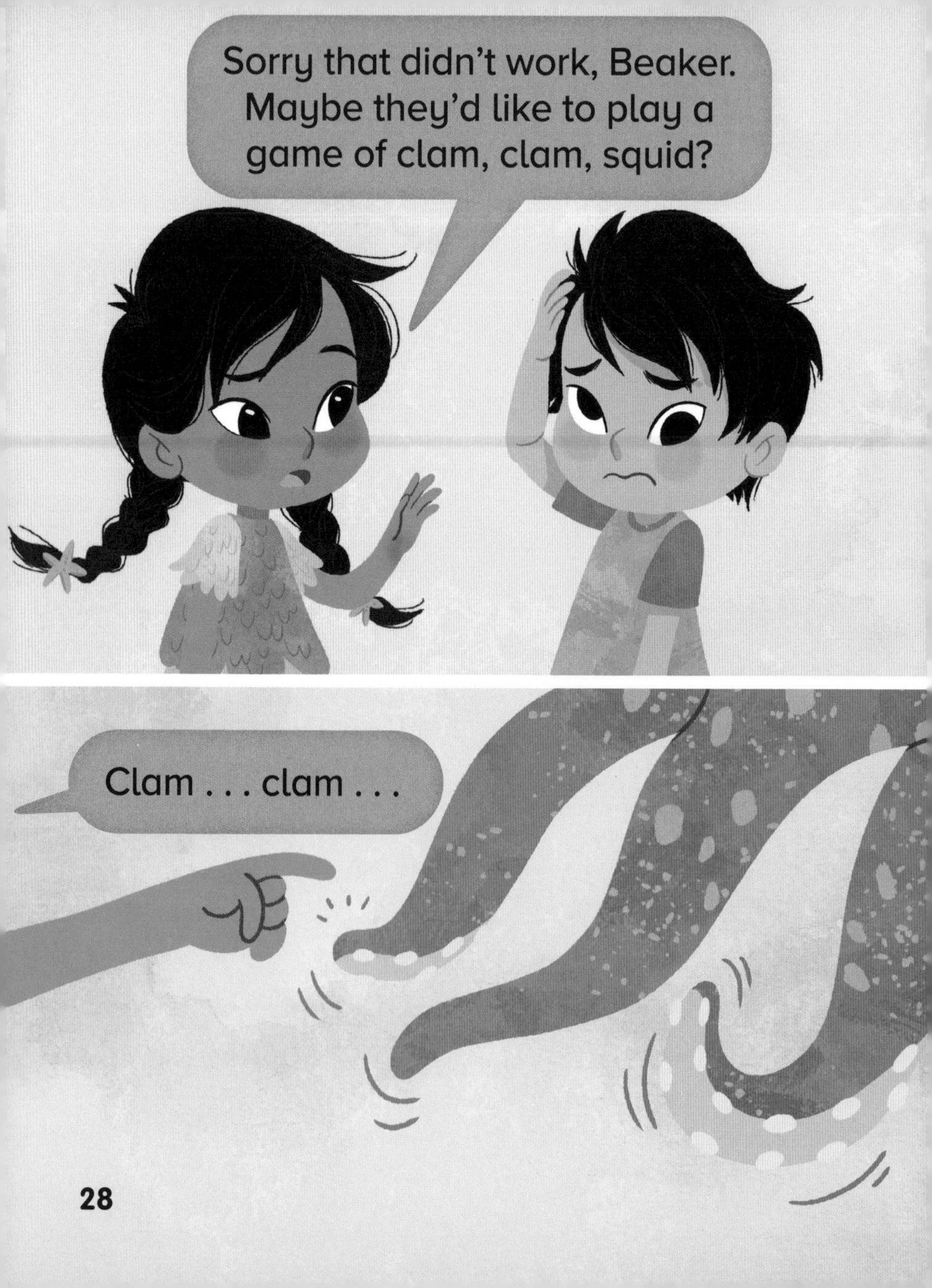
Sorry that didn't work, Beaker. Maybe they'd like to play a game of clam, clam, squid?
Clam . . . clam . . .

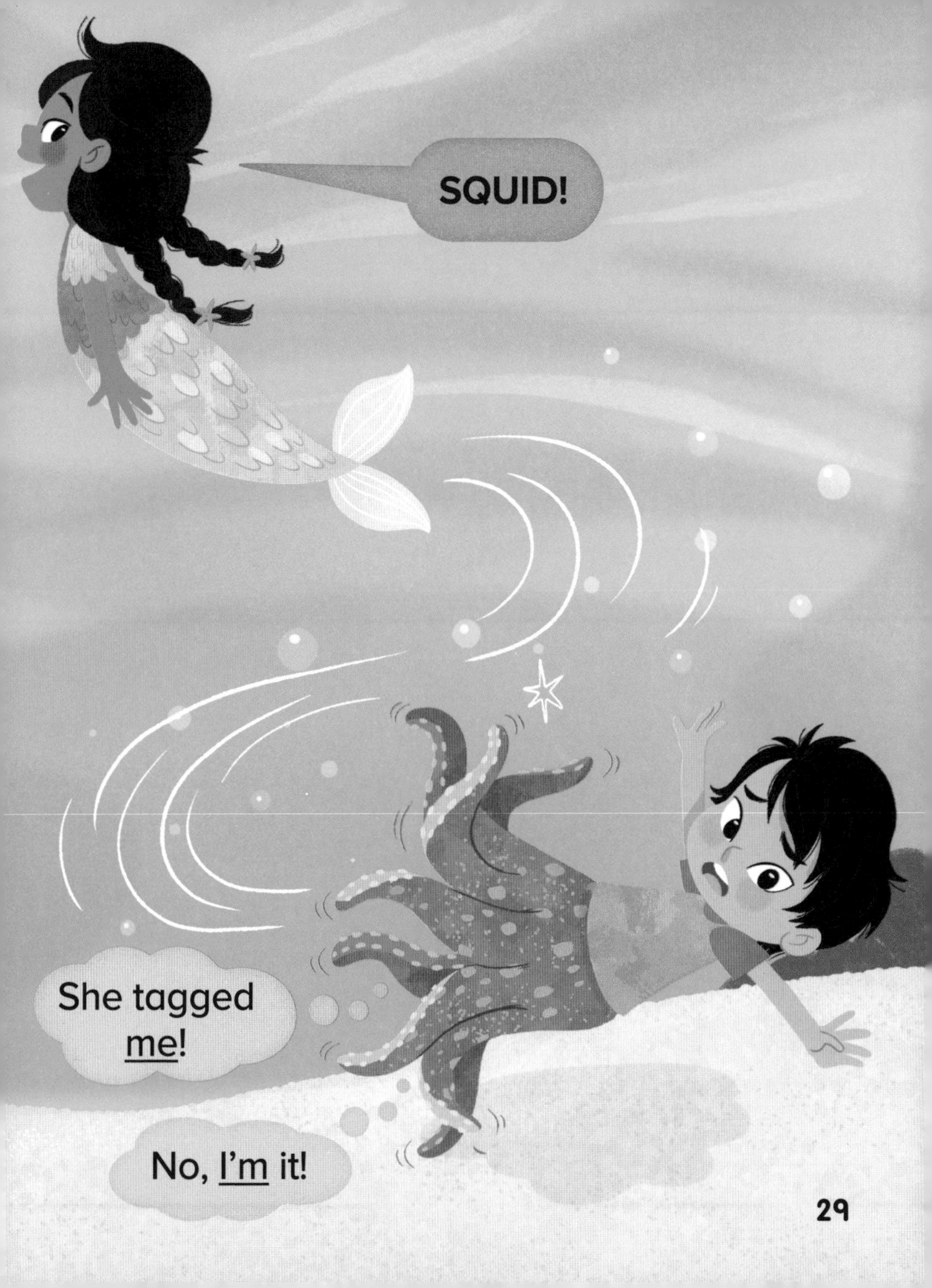
SQUID!
She tagged me!
No, I'm it!

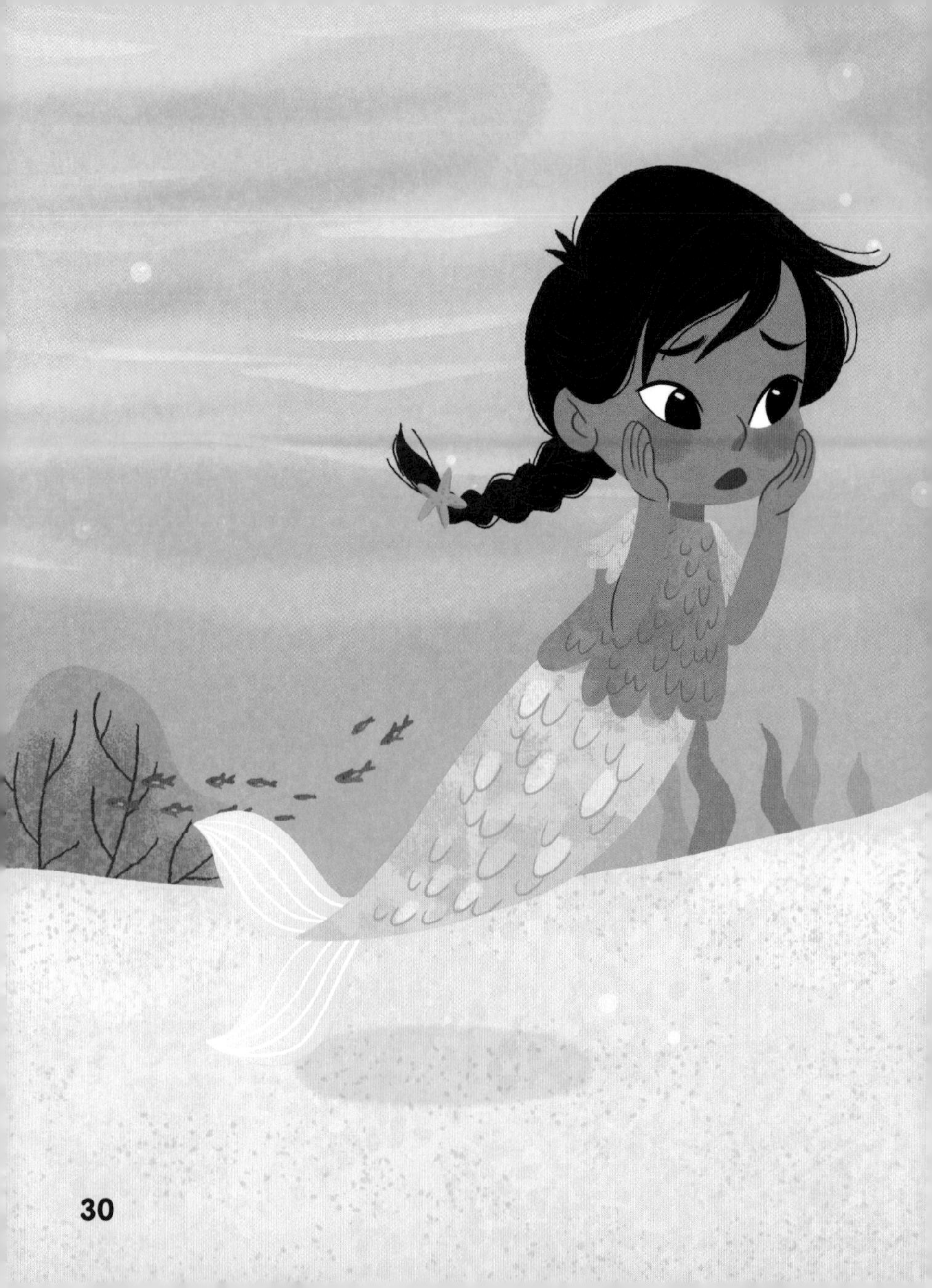

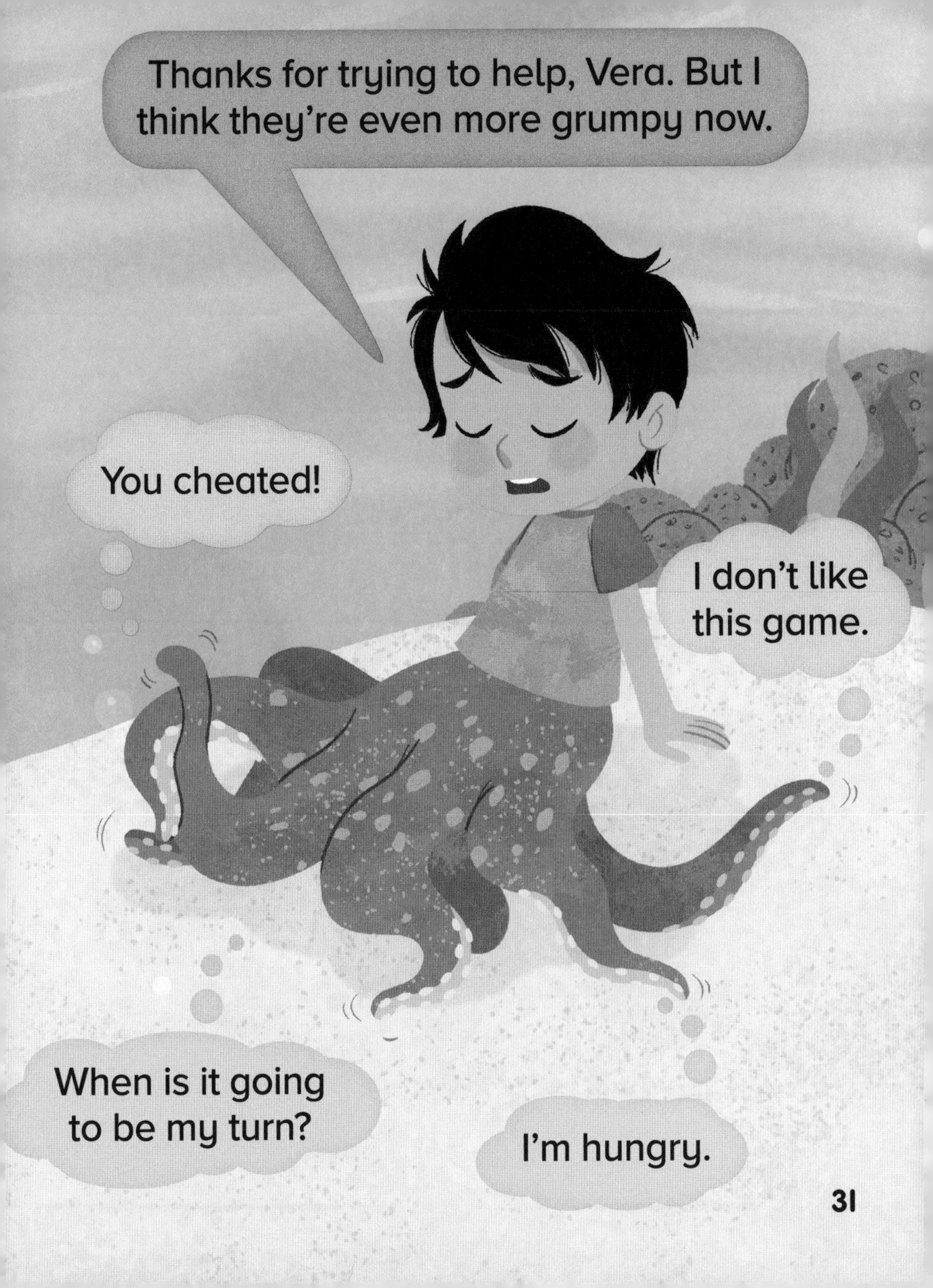
Thanks for trying to help, Vera. But I think they're even more grumpy now.
You cheated!
I don't like this game.
When is it going to be my turn?
I'm hungry.

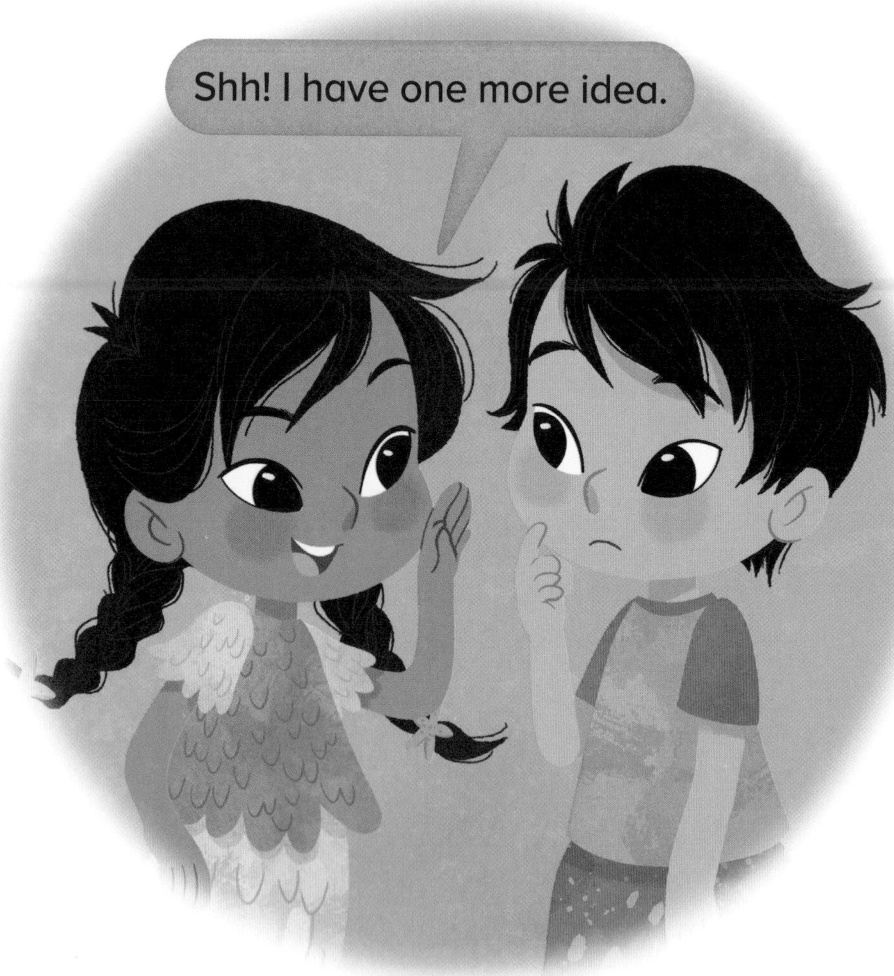
Shh! I have one more idea.

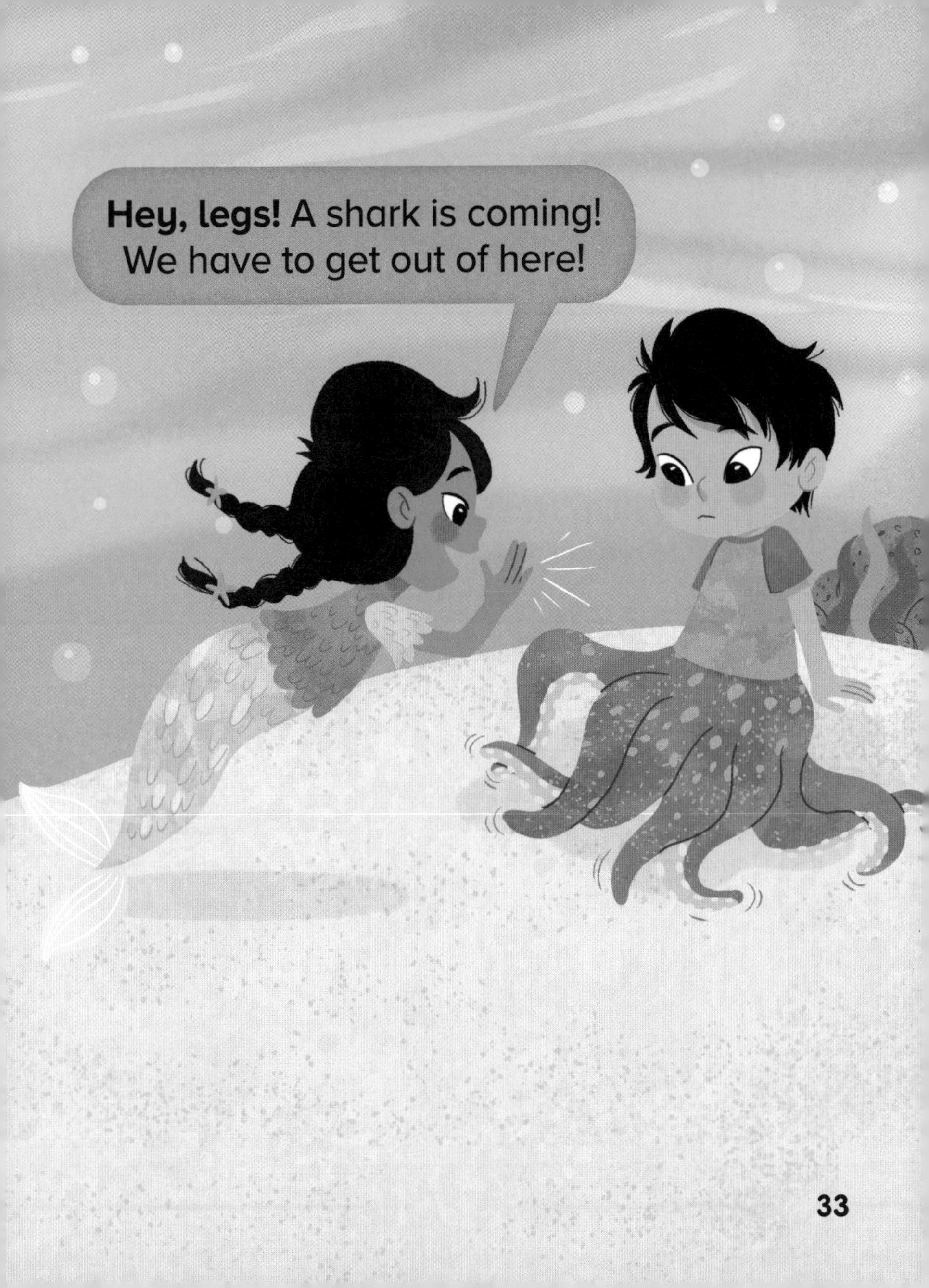
Hey, legs! A shark is coming! We have to get out of here!

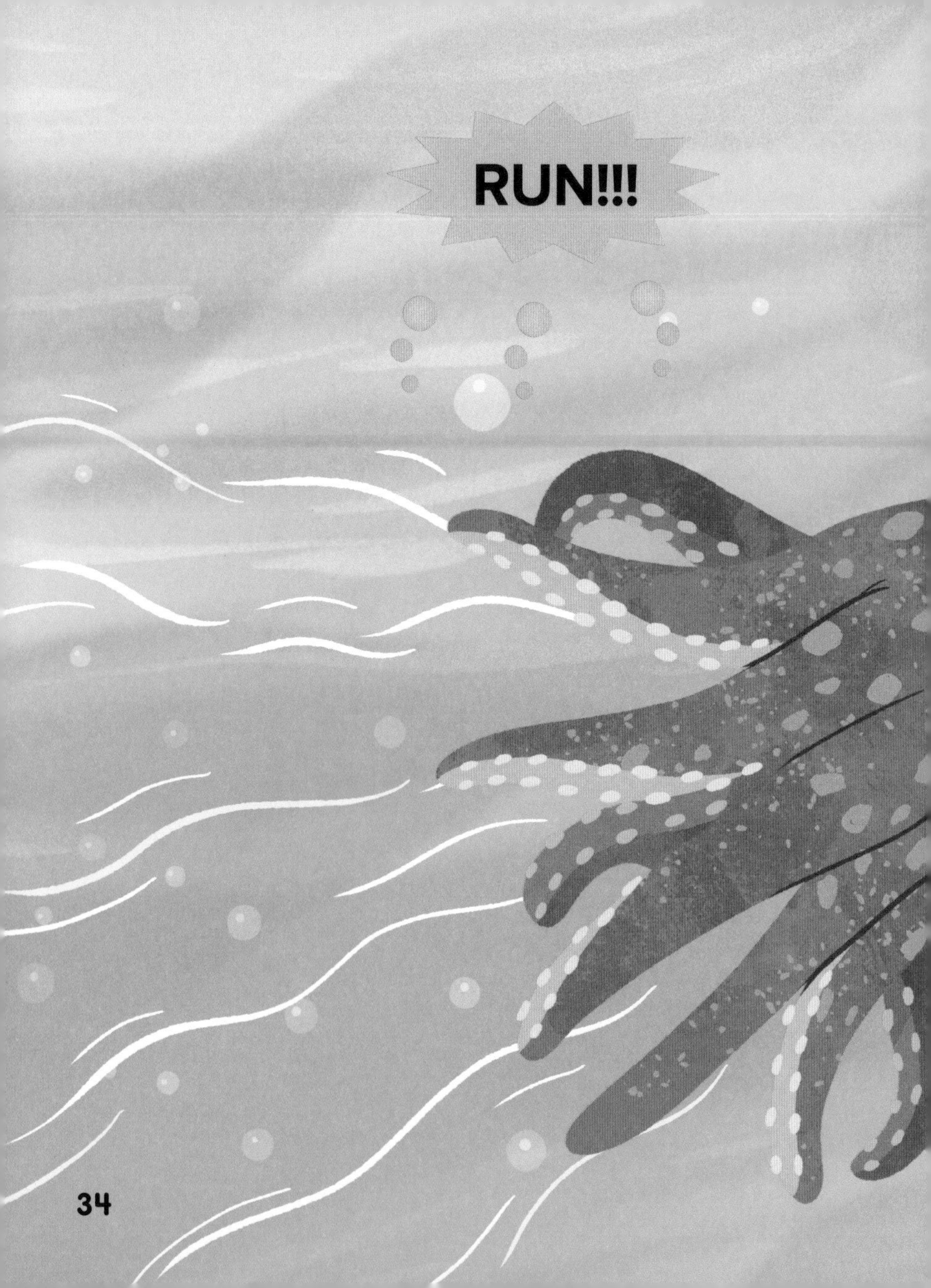
RUN!!!

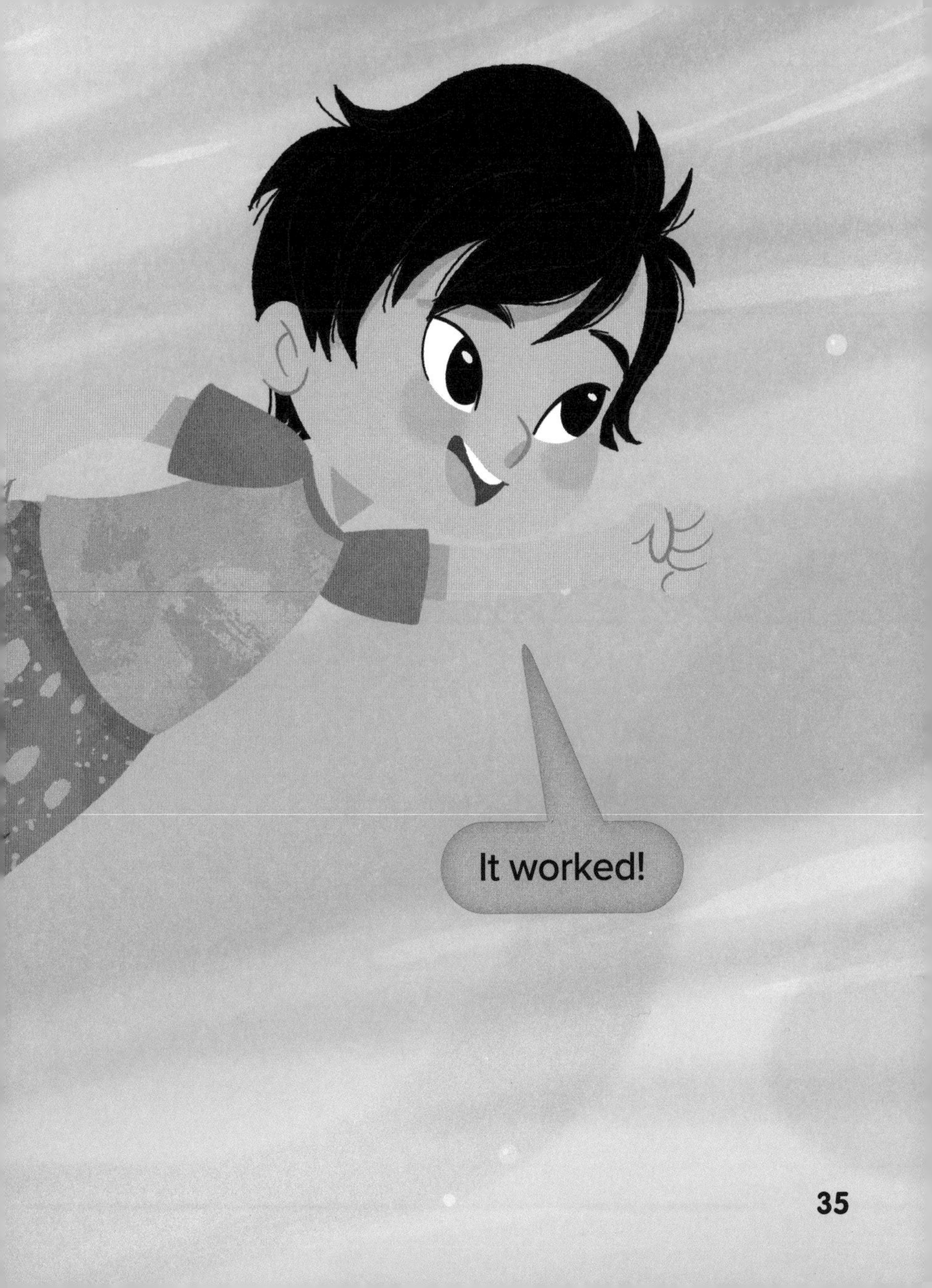
It worked!

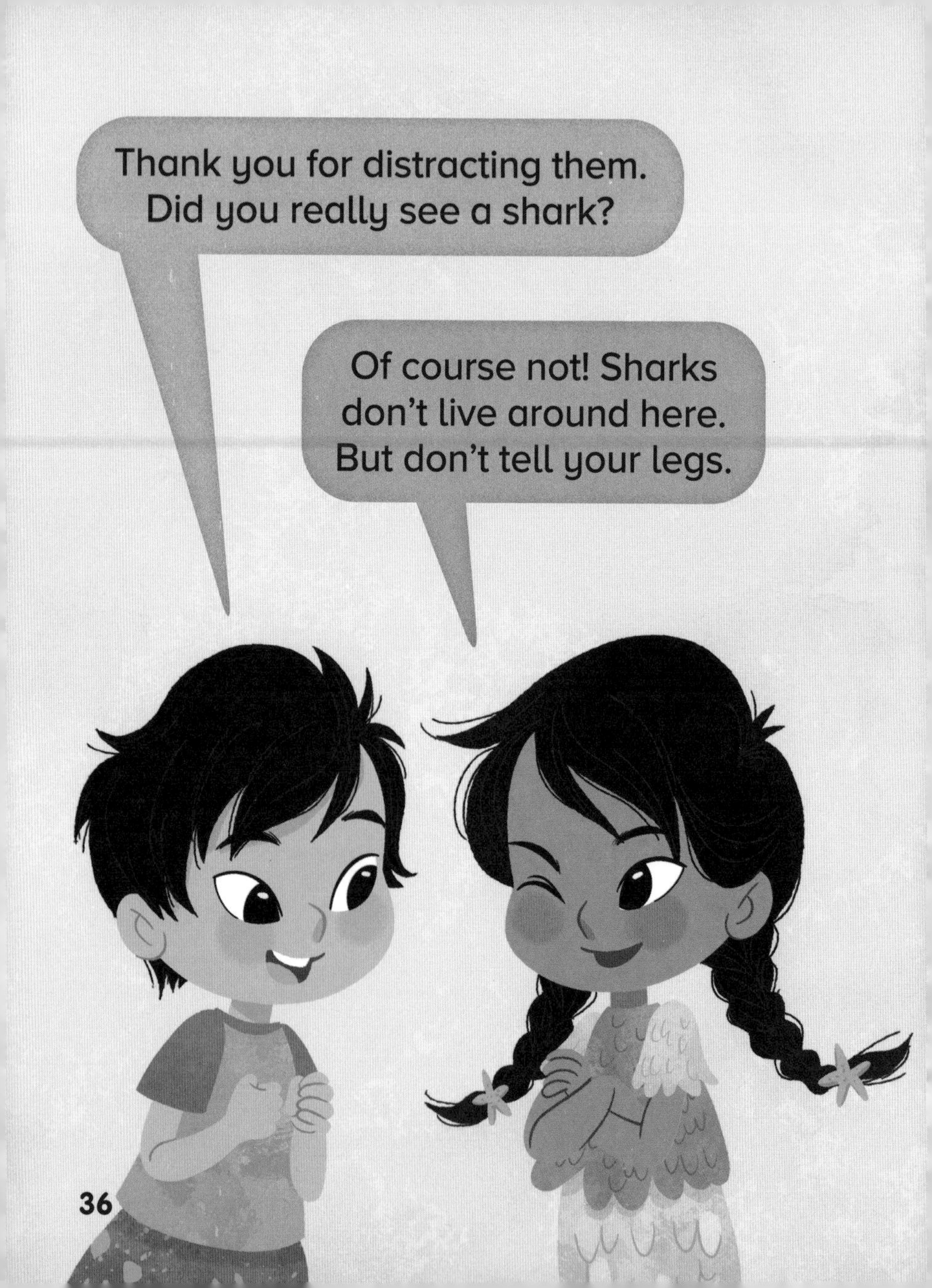
Thank you for distracting them. Did you really see a shark?
Of course not! Sharks don't live around here. But don't tell your legs.

A TIGHT SQUEEZE

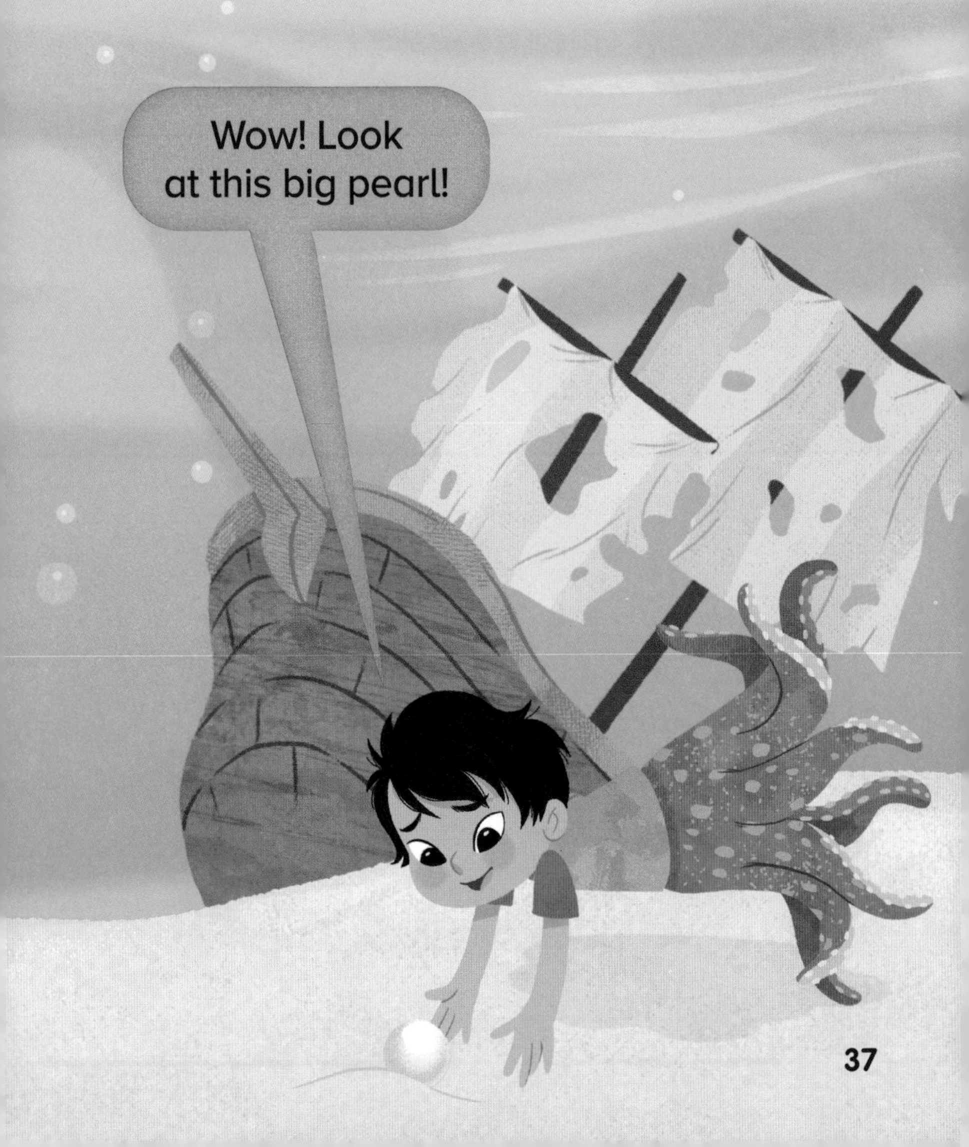
Wow! Look at this big pearl!

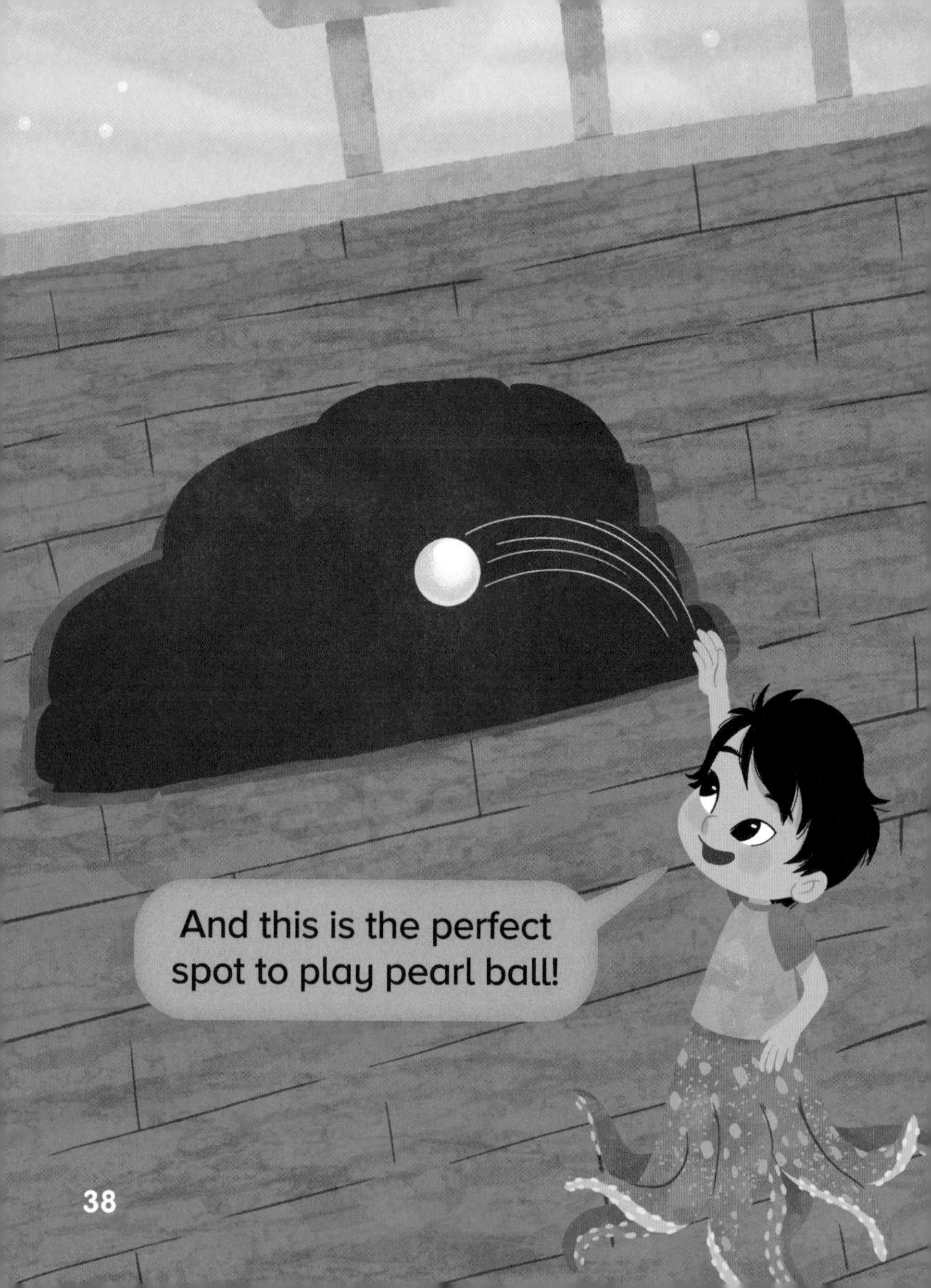
And this is the perfect spot to play pearl ball!

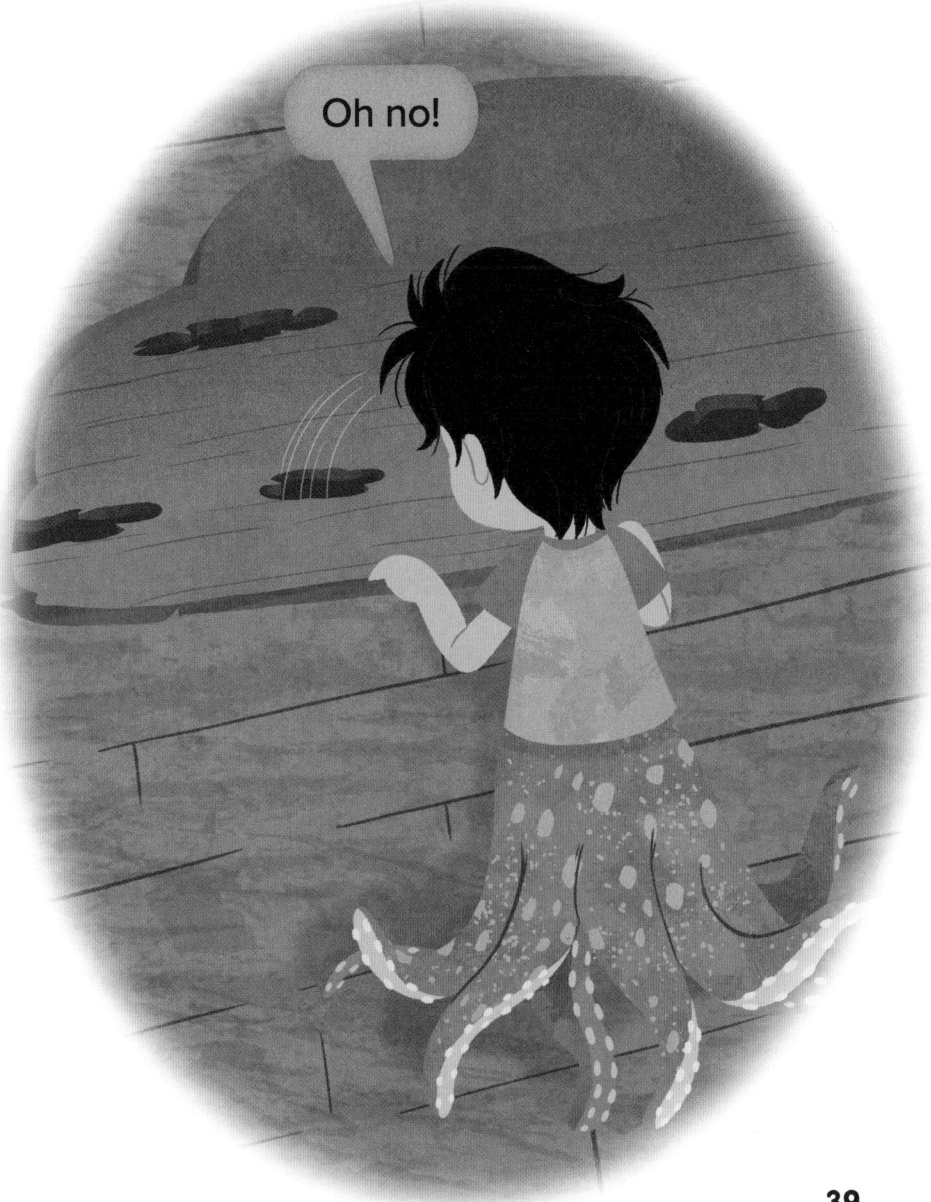
Oh no!

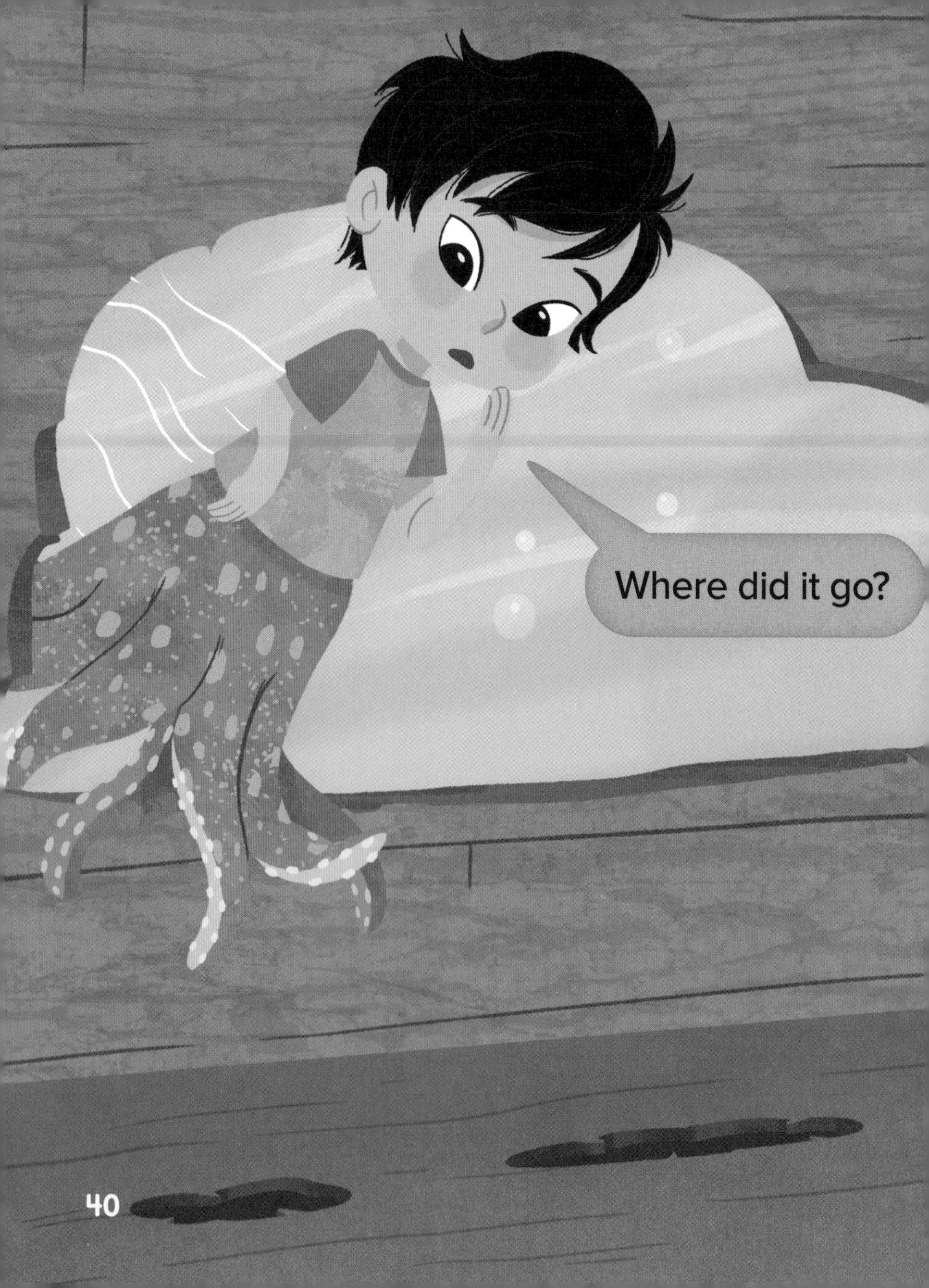
Where did it go?

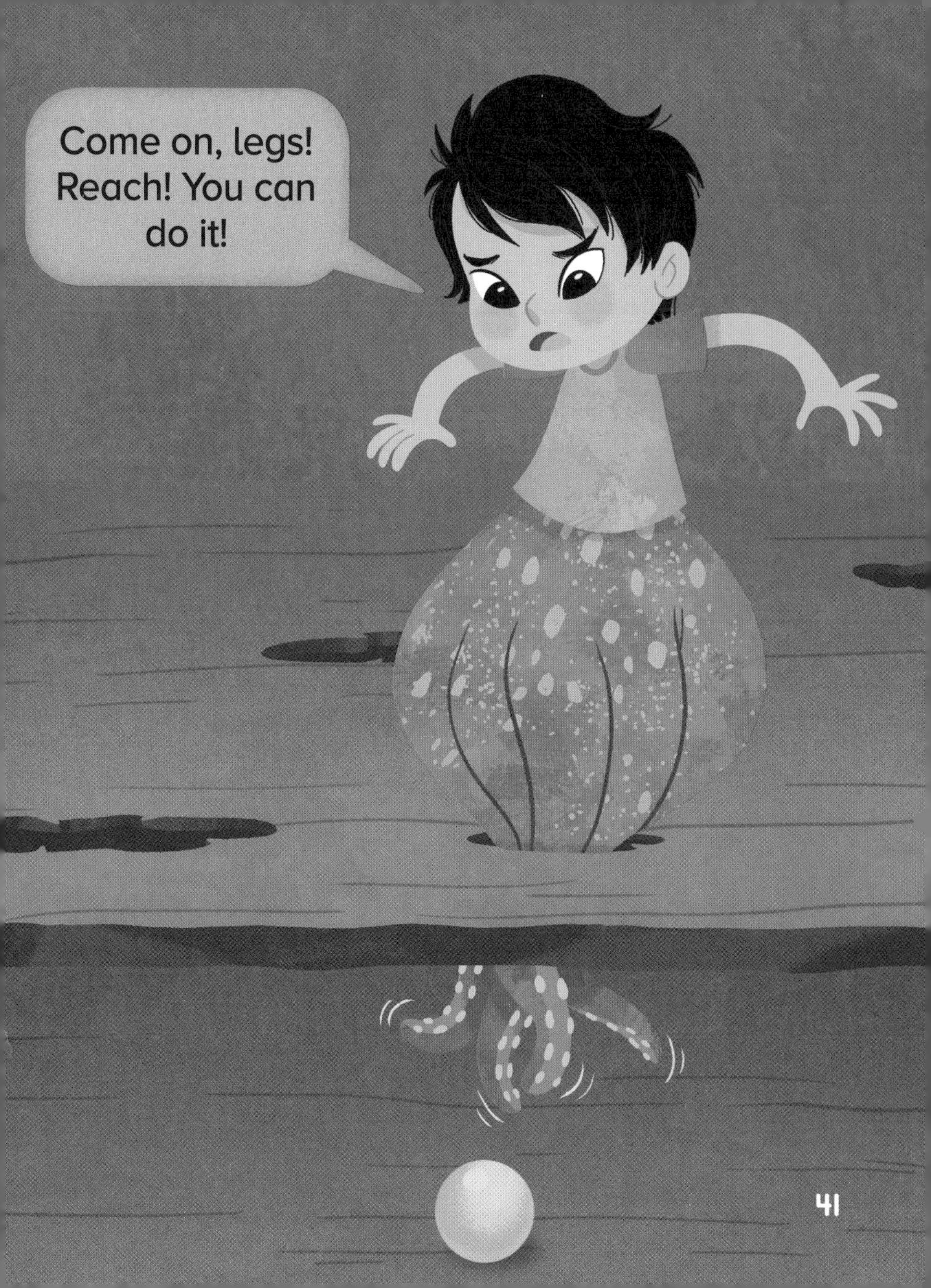
Come on, legs! Reach! You can do it!

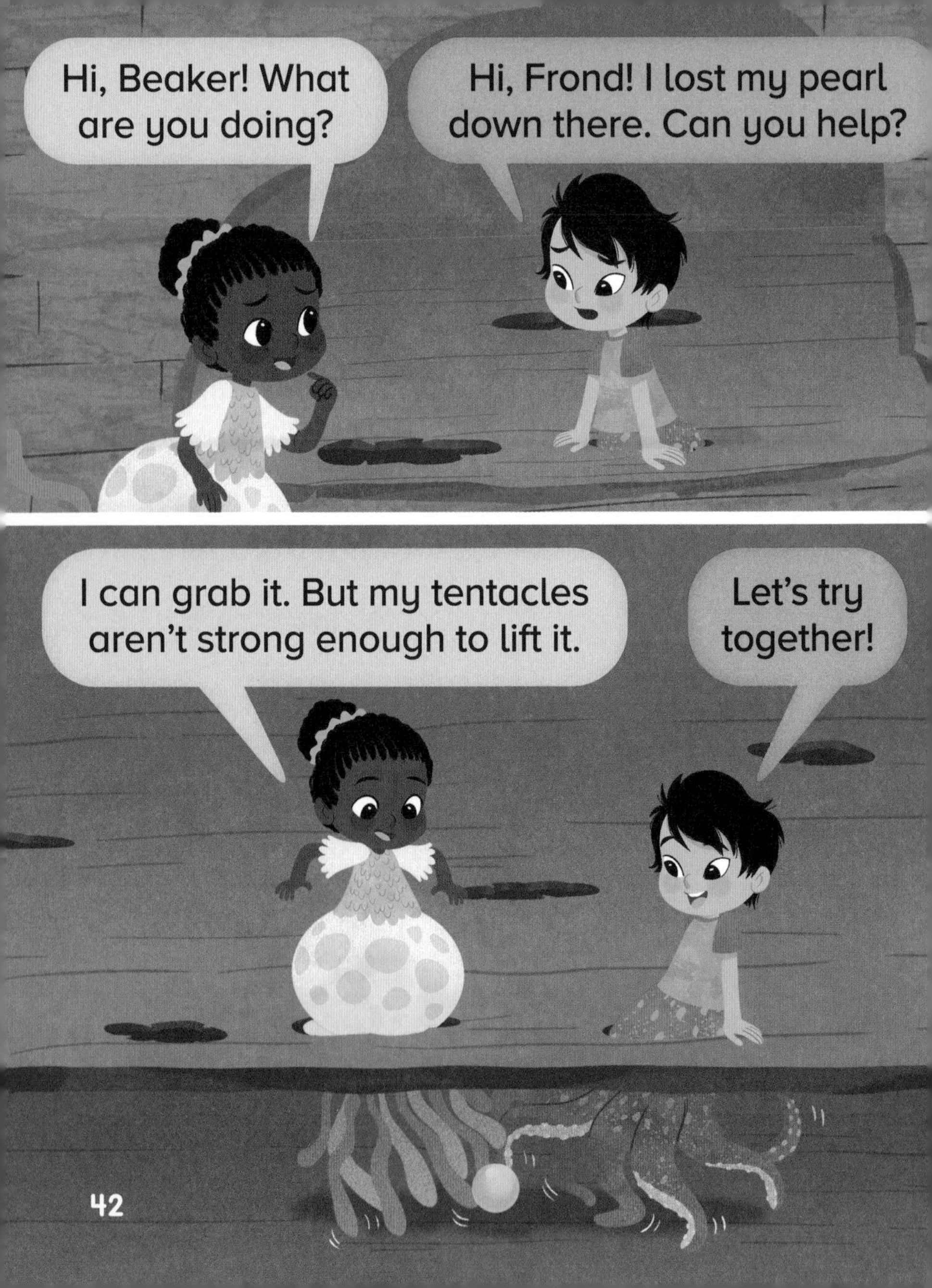
Hi, Beaker! What are you doing?
Hi, Frond! I lost my pearl down there. Can you help?
I can grab it. But my tentacles aren't strong enough to lift it.
Let's try together!

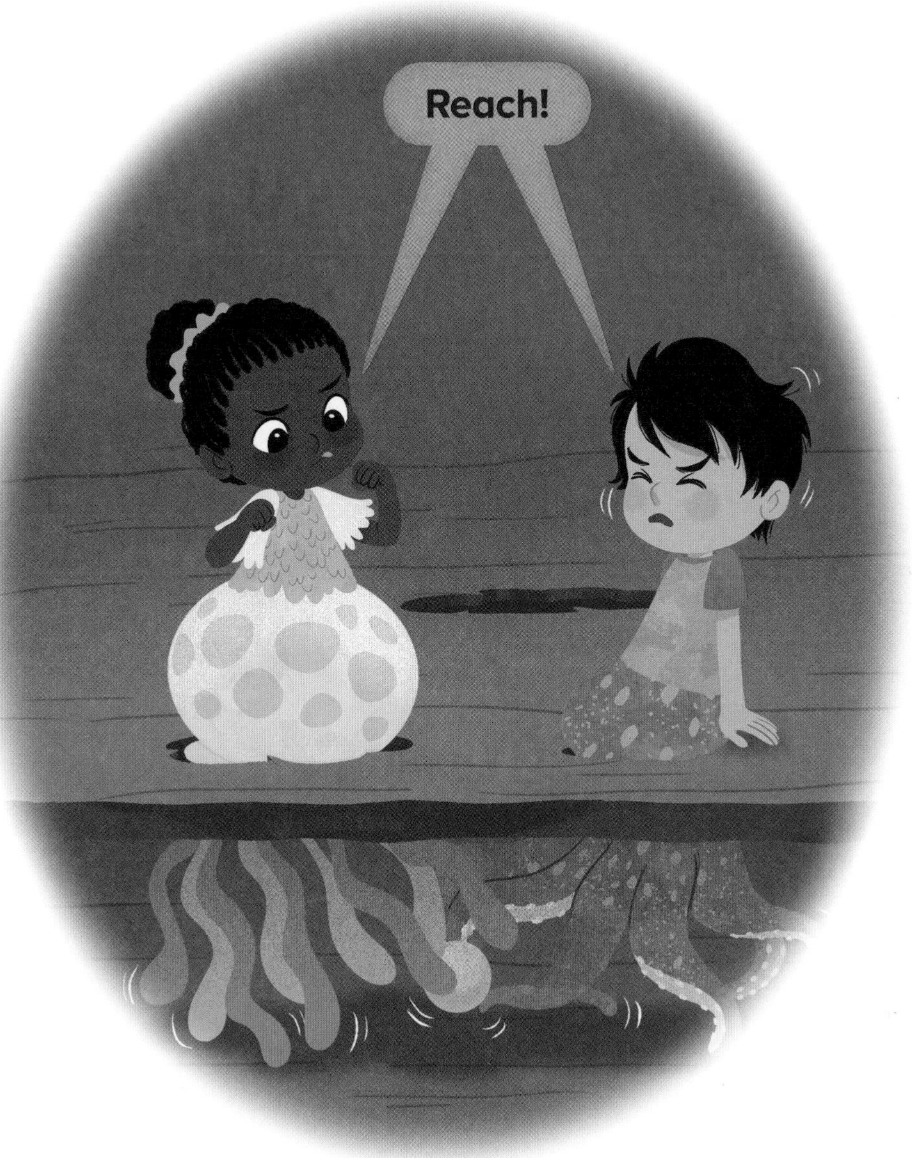
Reach!

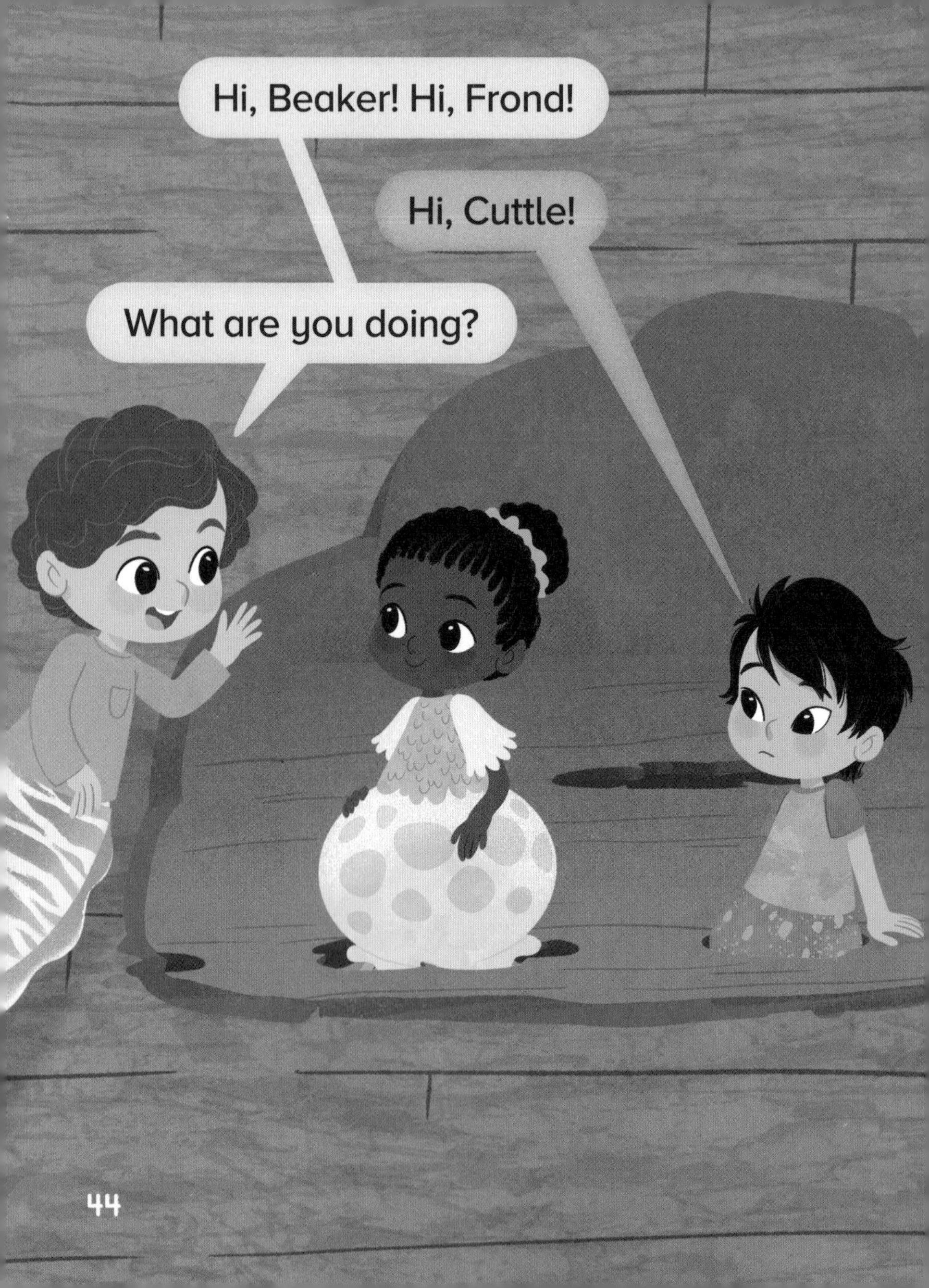
Hi, Beaker! Hi, Frond!
Hi, Cuttle!
What are you doing?

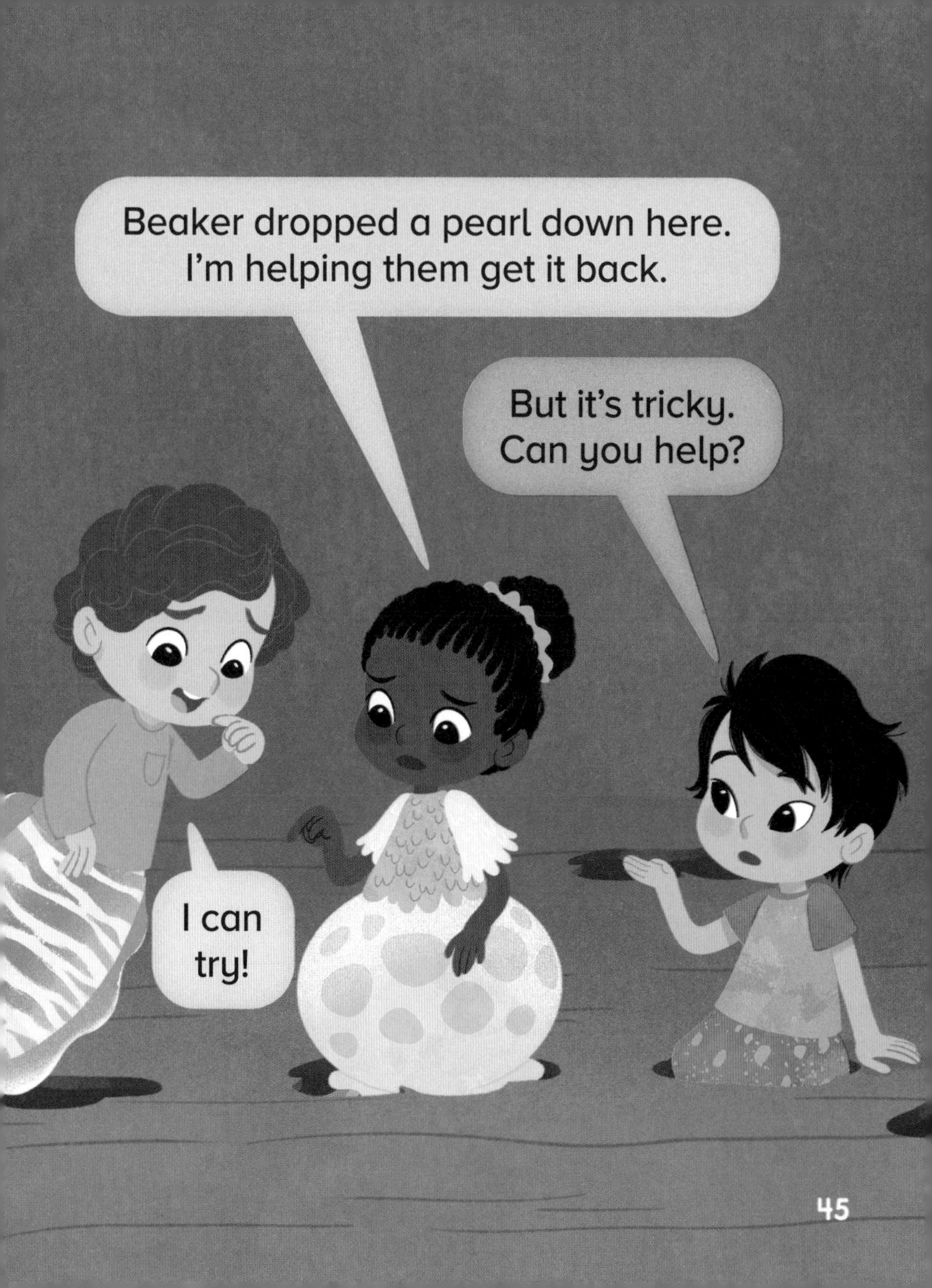
Beaker dropped a pearl down here. I'm helping them get it back.
But it's tricky. Can you help?
I can try!

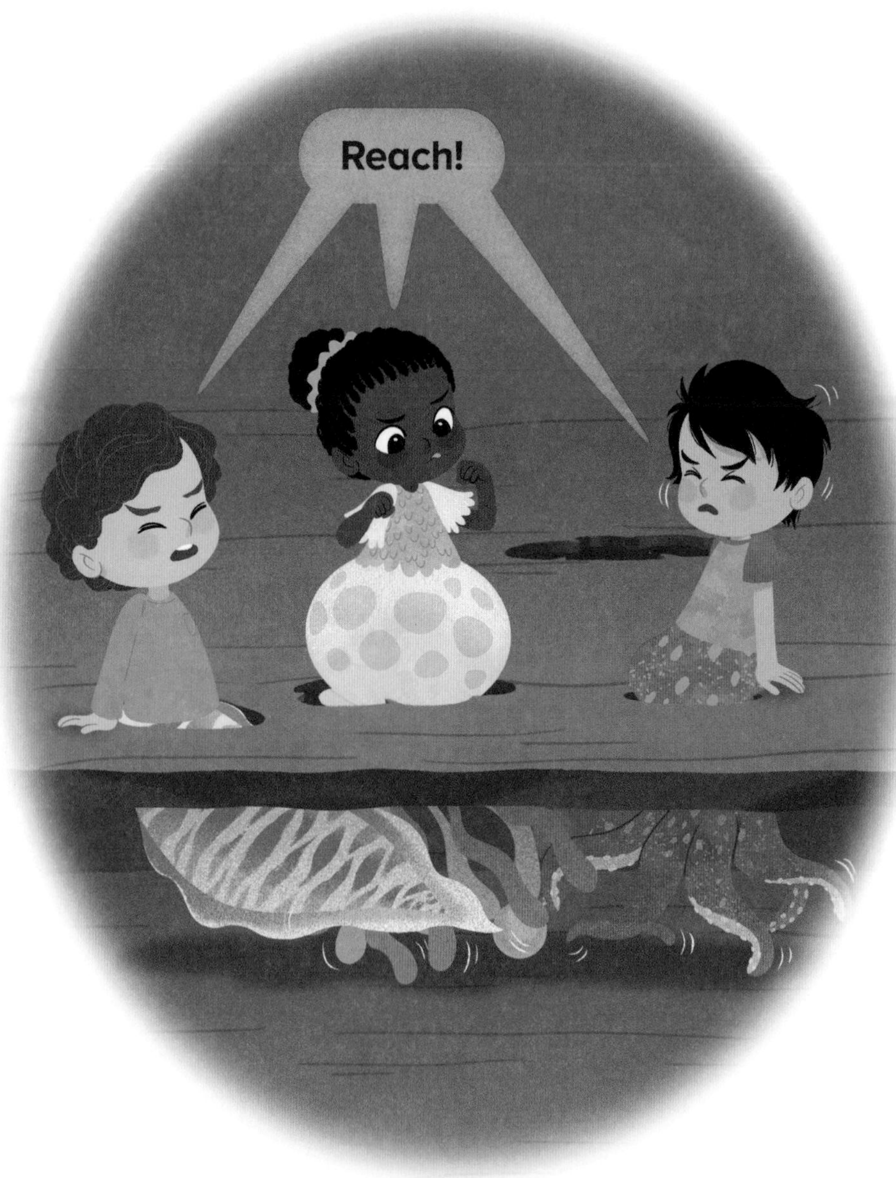
Reach!

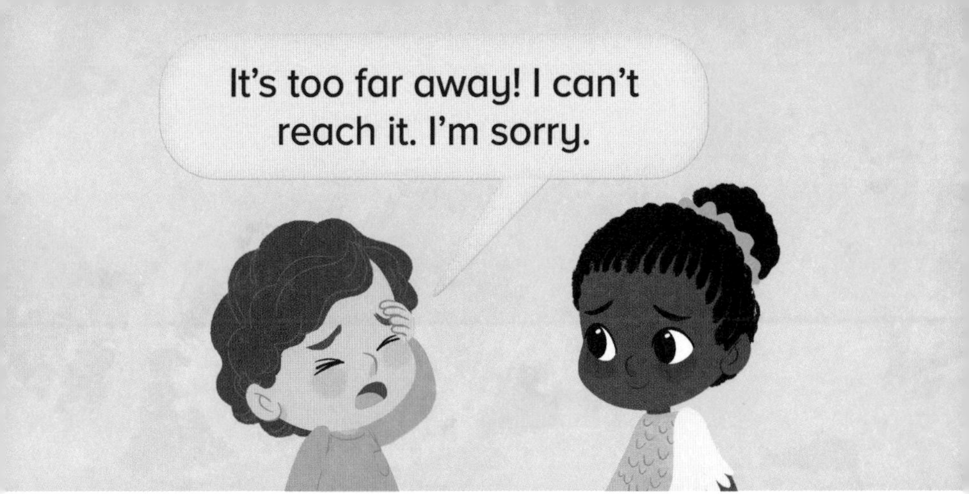
It's too far away! I can't reach it. I'm sorry.

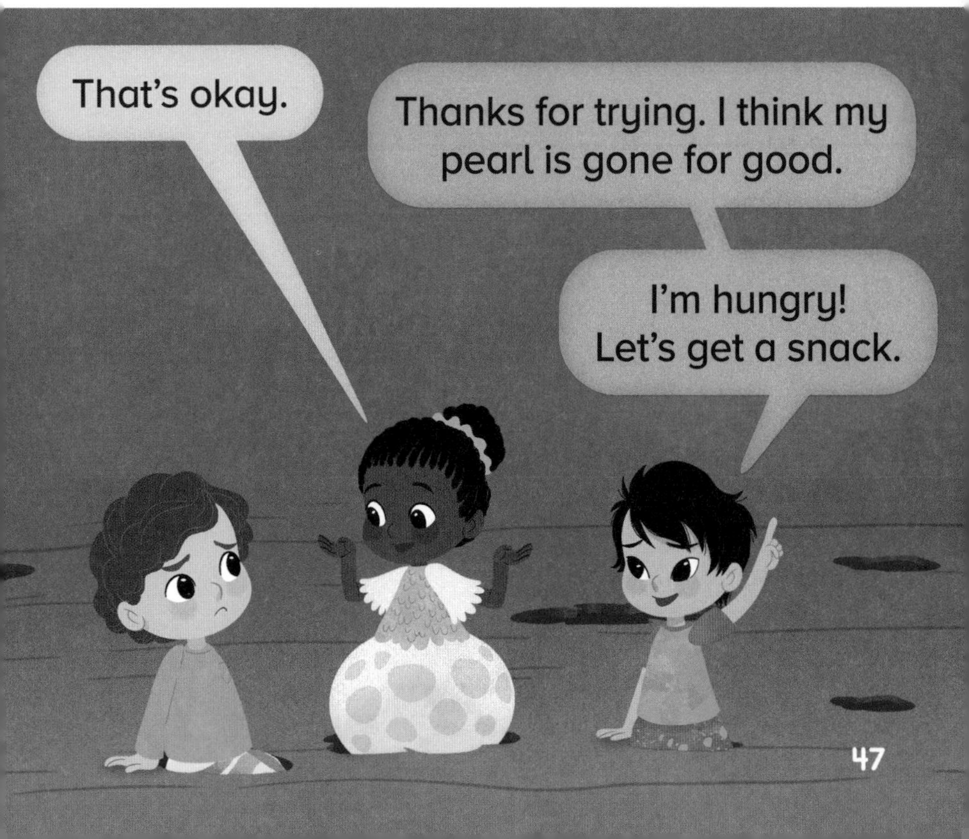
That's okay.
Thanks for trying. I think my pearl is gone for good.
I'm hungry! Let's get a snack.

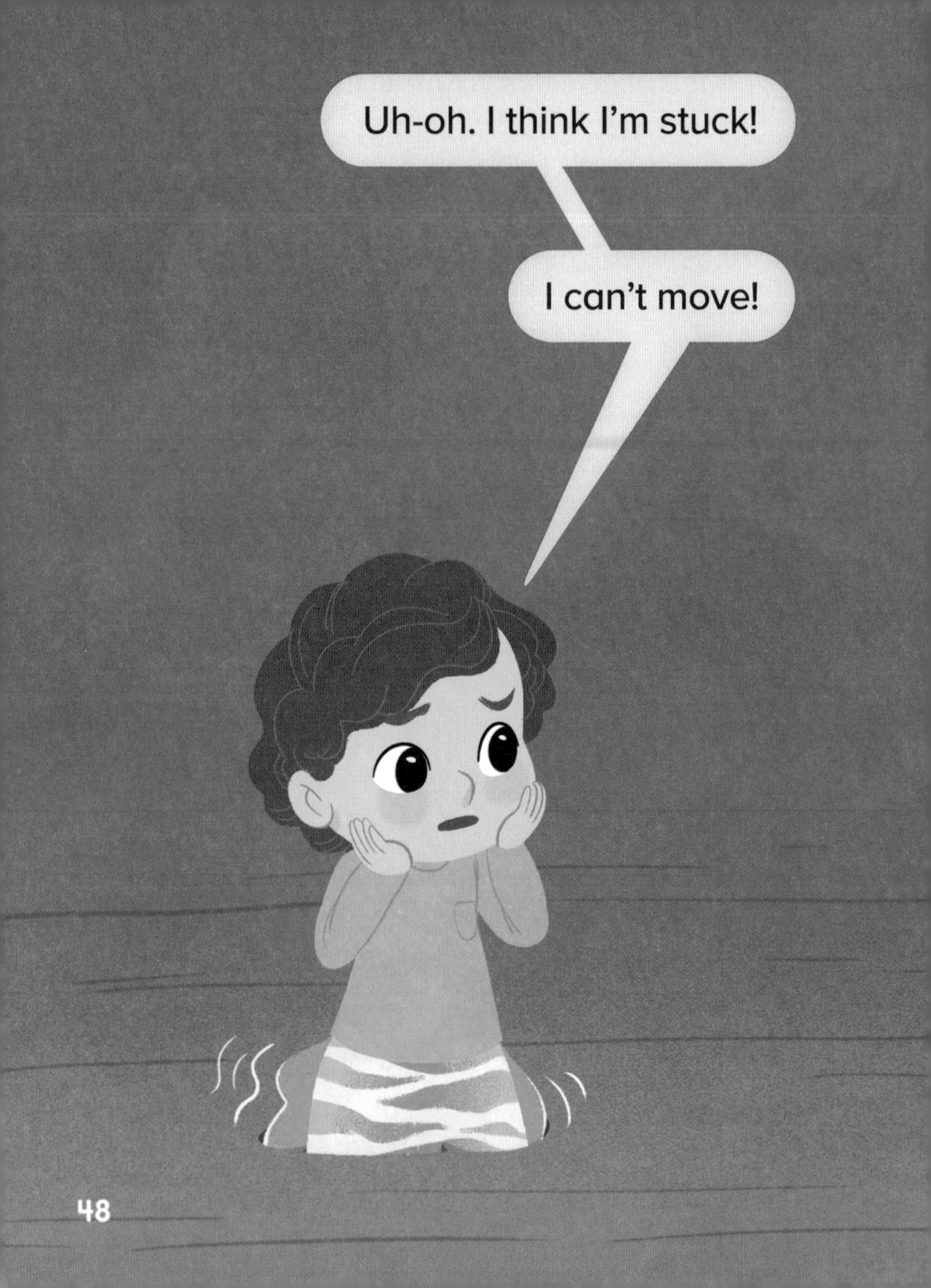
Uh-oh. I think I'm stuck!
I can't move!

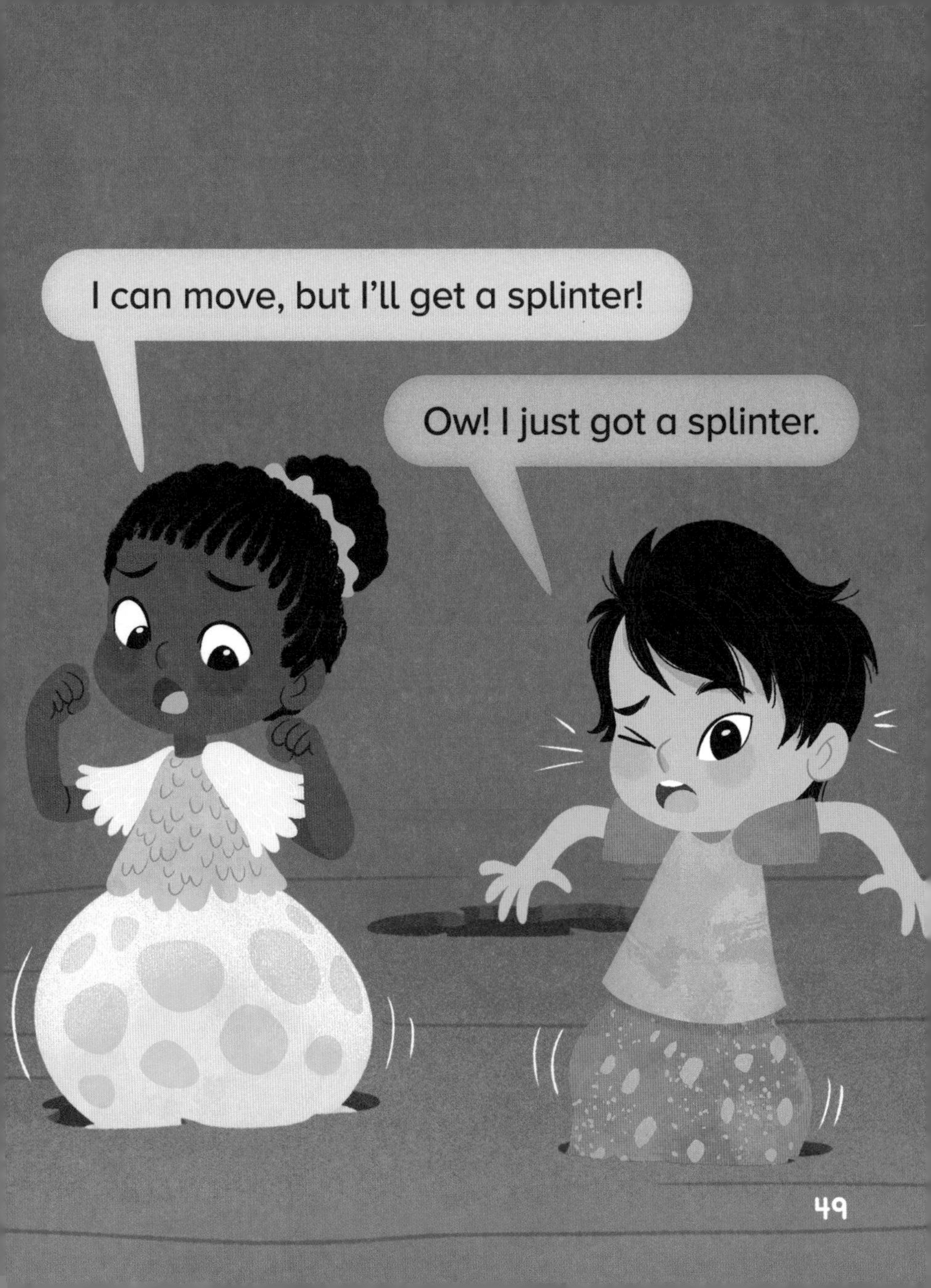
I can move, but I'll get a splinter!
Ow! I just got a splinter.

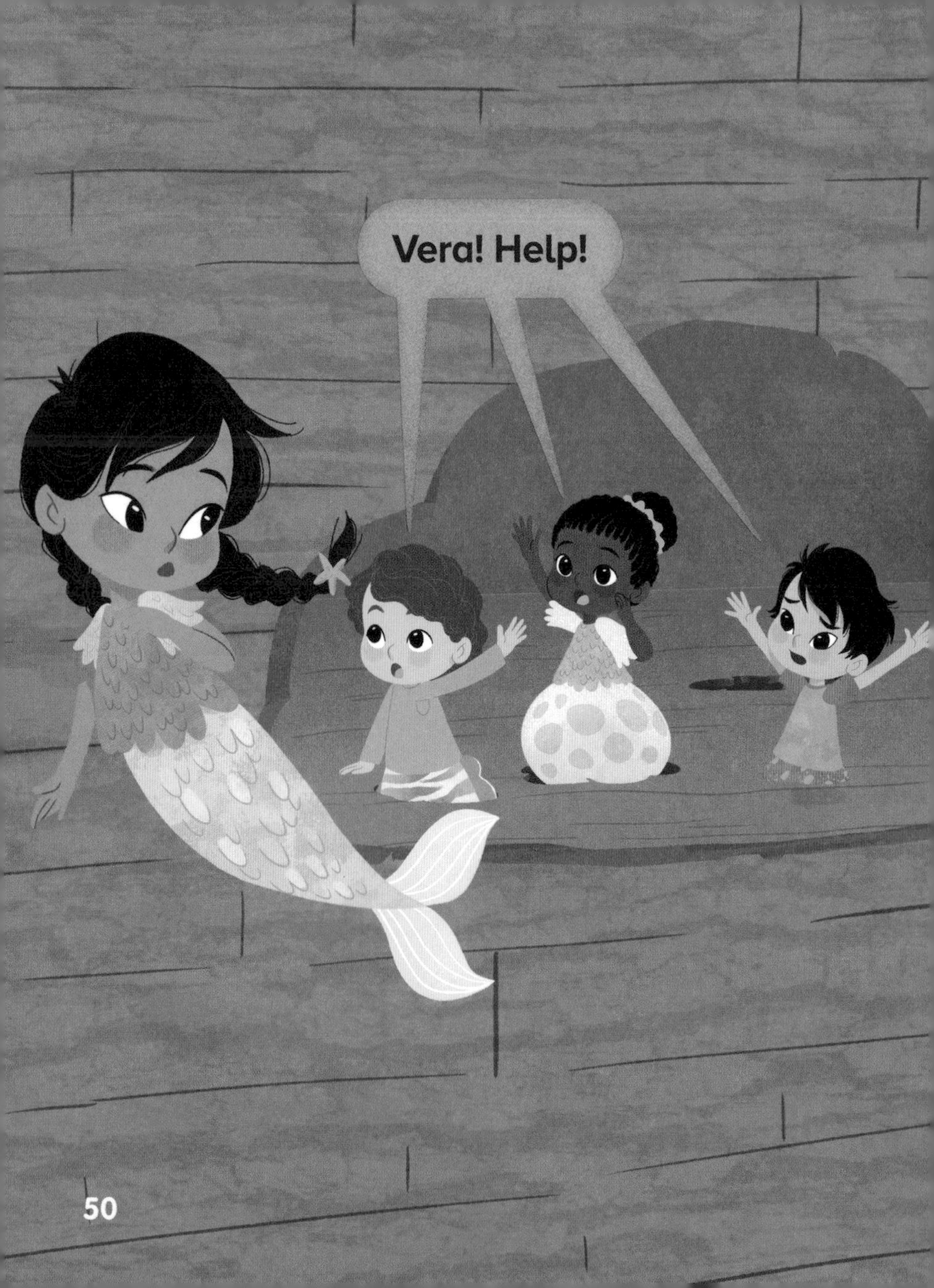
Vera! Help!

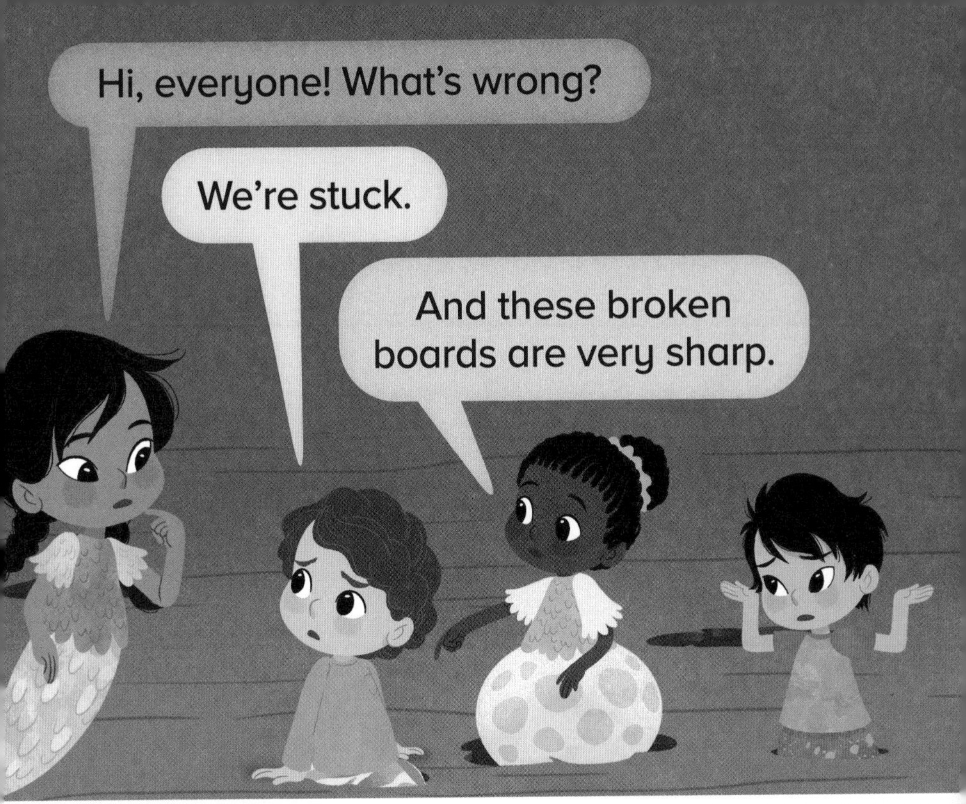
Hi, everyone! What's wrong?
We're stuck.
And these broken boards are very sharp.

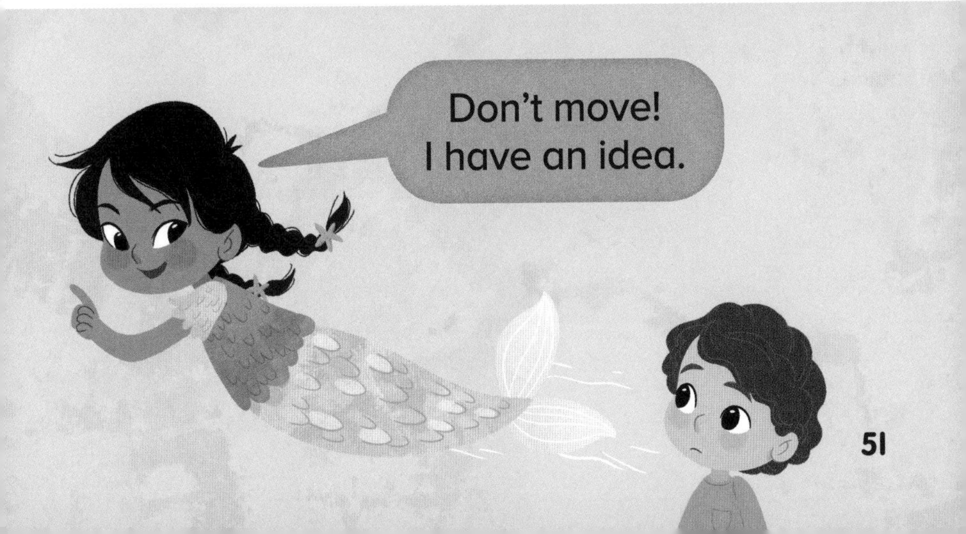
Don't move! I have an idea.

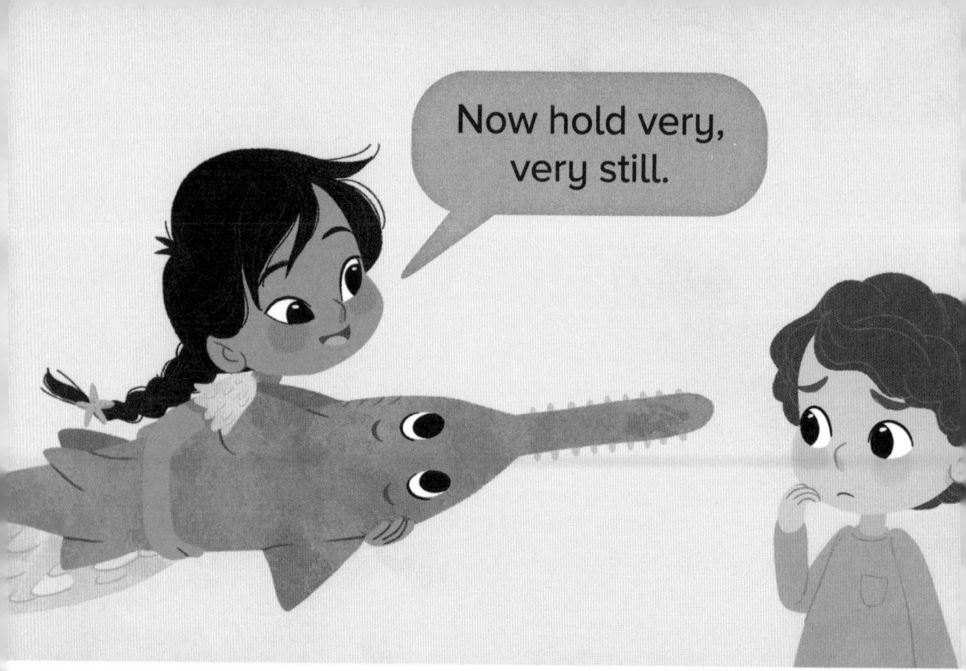
Now hold very,
very still.

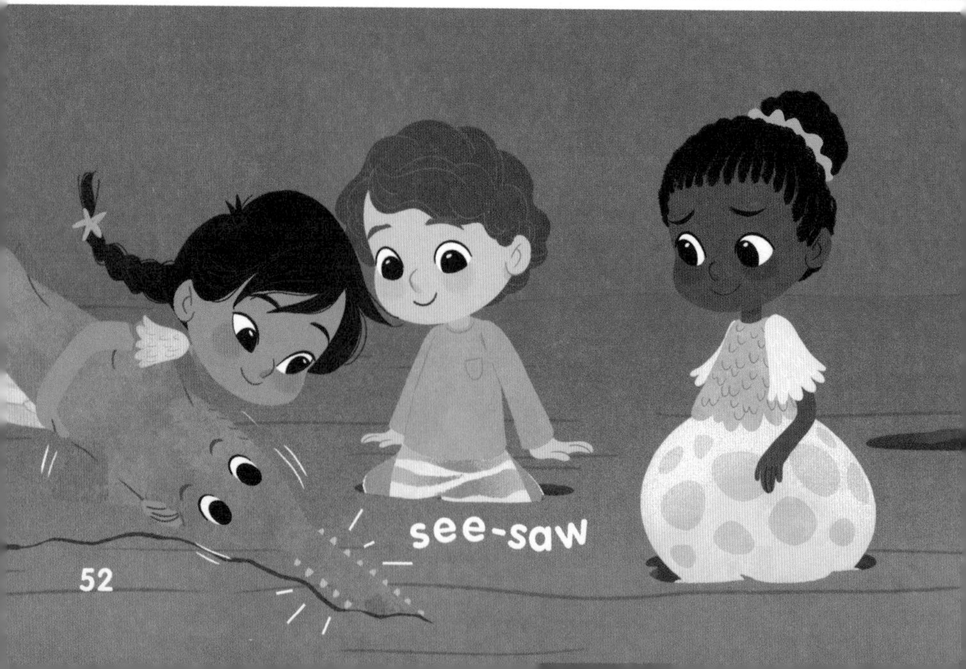
see-saw

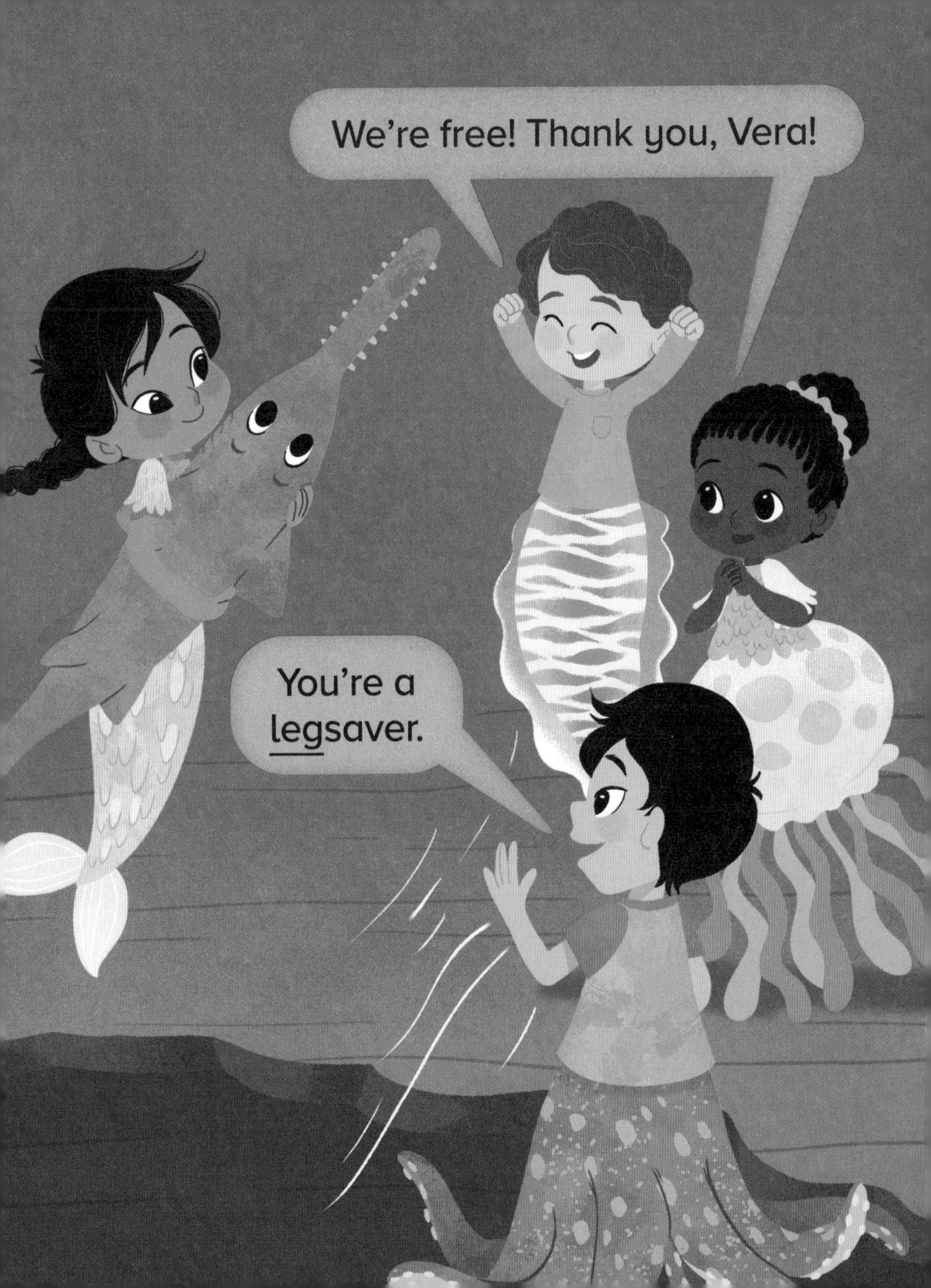
We're free! Thank you, Vera!
You're a legsaver.

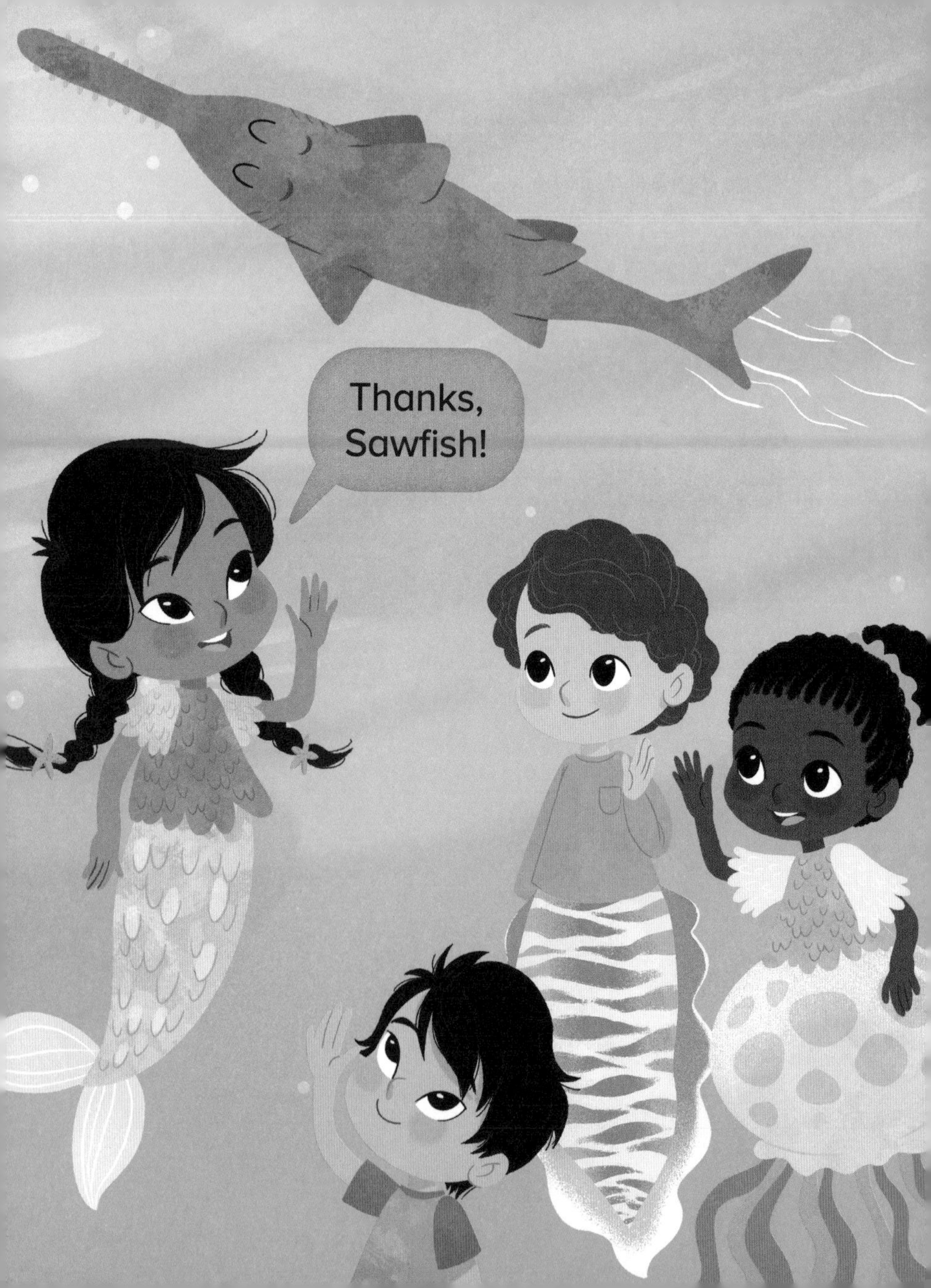
Thanks, Sawfish!

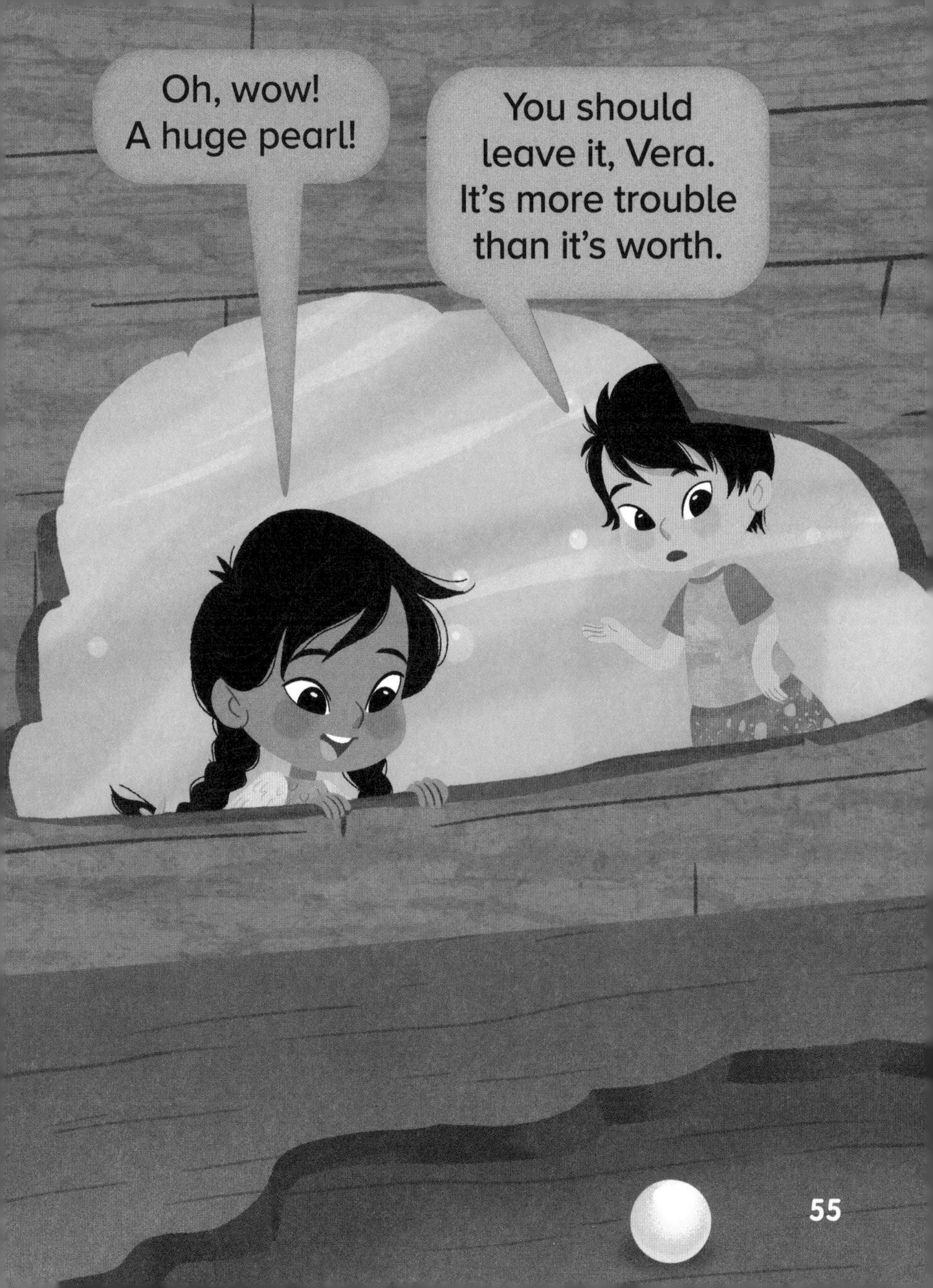
Oh, wow! A huge pearl!
You should leave it, Vera. It's more trouble than it's worth.

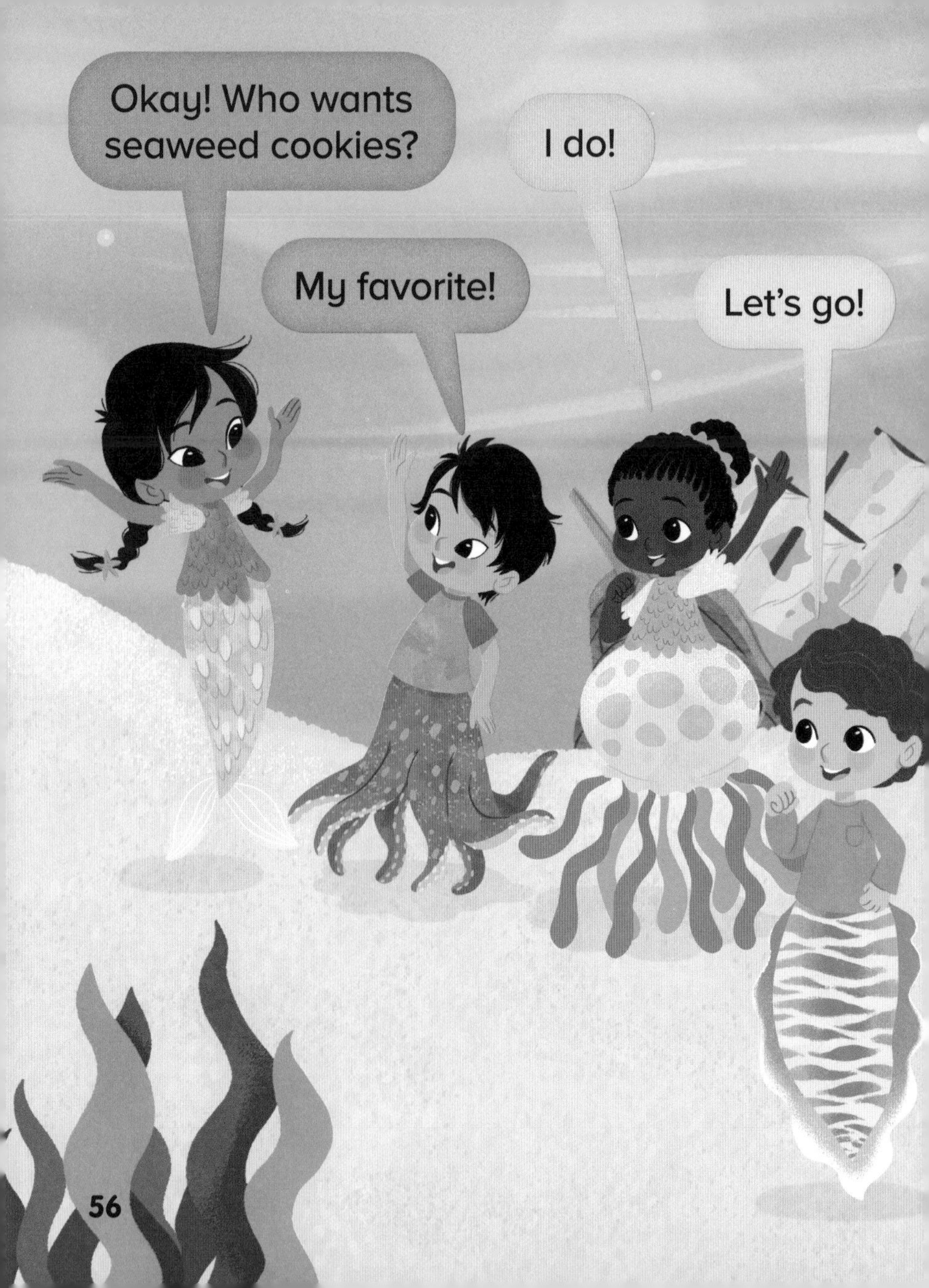
Okay! Who wants seaweed cookies?
I do!
My favorite!
Let's go!

ABOUT THE CREATORS

KYLE LUKOFF has never met a mermaid. He would very much like to be friends with an octopus! But he would rather climb trees than go to the beach, and he would rather write books for kids than learn how to scuba dive. He is the Stonewall award-winning author of lots of books, including WHEN AIDAN BECAME A BROTHER and TOO BRIGHT TO SEE.

KAT UNO was born, raised, and currently resides in Hawaii. Living on an island surrounded by the beautiful Pacific Ocean has always provided much inspiration. Kat has loved being creative ever since she was little. She enjoys illustrating children's books, and mermaids are one of her favorite subjects to draw! She is also a proud mom of two eager readers.

YOU CAN DRAW VERA!

1 Draw the outline of Vera's head, torso, and tail.

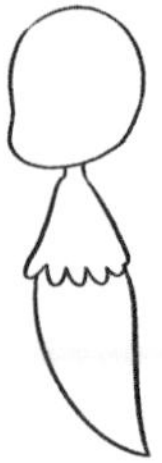

2 Add her arms and ear. Finish her tail.

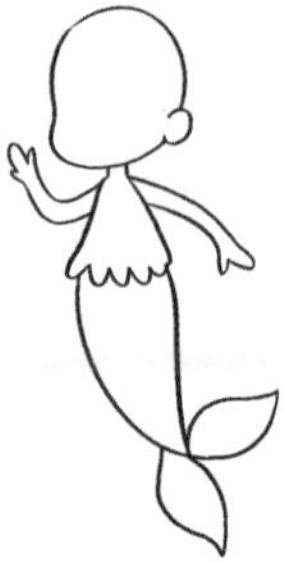

3 Draw her hair.

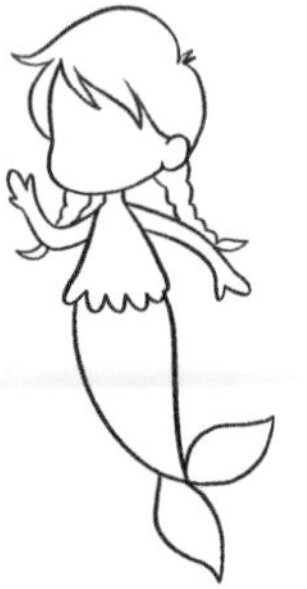

4 Add her scales and her short sleeves.

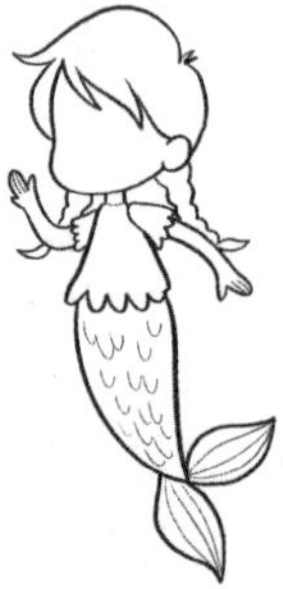

5 Draw Vera's face and add details to her hair.

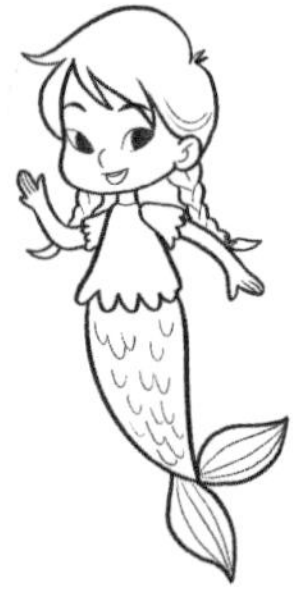

6 Color in your drawing!

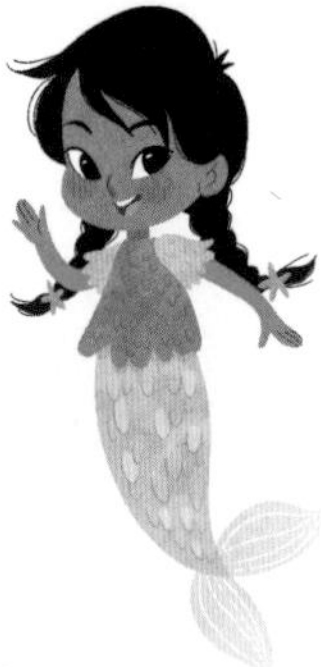

WHAT'S YOUR STORY?

Beaker plays pearl ball in the sunken ship.
Imagine that **you** are playing underwater!
What game would you play?
What would you play with?
Write and draw your story!

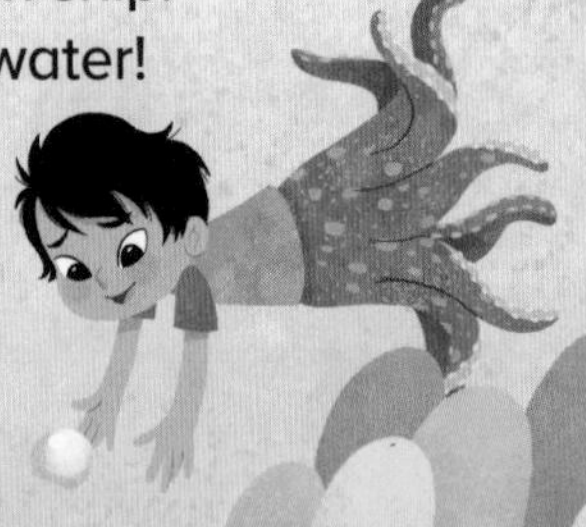